Edwin James

Wanderings of a Beauty

A Tale of the Real and the Ideal

Edwin James

Wanderings of a Beauty
A Tale of the Real and the Ideal

ISBN/EAN: 9783337030506

Printed in Europe, USA, Canada, Australia, Japan

Cover: Foto ©Andreas Hilbeck / pixelio.de

More available books at **www.hansebooks.com**

WANDERINGS OF A BEAUTY.

A Tale

OF

THE REAL AND THE IDEAL.

BY

MRS. EDWIN JAMES.

"O tu, cui feo la sorte
Dono infelice di belezza, ond'hai
Funesta dote, d'infiniti guai."

FILICAJA.

New-York:

Carleton, Publisher, 413 *Broadway.*

(LATE RUDD & CARLETON.)

M DCCC LXIII.

CONTENTS.

EVELYN TRAVERS;

OR,

WANDERINGS OF A BEAUTY.

———•◦•———

CHAPTER I.

INTRODUCTORY.

ALTHOUGH linked by no ties of kindred to the fair subject of this biographical sketch, the author may at least claim to have loved her with a love passing that of a sister—to have fully appreciated her rare endowments of mind and person, and, alas! to have had too frequent occasion to chide her girlish follies, and, in after life, to weep over her more womanly failings. Beauty has ever, and justly, been styled "a fatal gift." From the classic Helen to the lovely and unhappy Mary Stuart, and in more modern times the matchless and queenly Antoinette of France all these, and others of lesser note, have furnished us with abundant examples of the cruel destiny of those who possess this much coveted distinction. For my part, I can only be too thankful for having been endowed by nature with a face which the most indulgent of my friends could but term pleasing, and which a casual acquaintance might call plain. Enemies I never had; I was not sufficiently handsome.

When I first met Evelyn Travers we were both inmates of a Parisian "Pension de demoiselles." Although four years my junior, her precocious intellect and superior talents led her to prefer the society of the elder girls to that of those of her own age. Our mutual passion for music threw us constantly together, and another circumstance contributed still further to cement a friendship which has never since diminished. We were both alone in the world. My own beloved parents I had lost. My father fell in India, in the field, and my brokenhearted mother only survived her voyage homeward to expire in the arms of her only child. It was at that time of bitter trial, that the loving devotion of Evelyn to her friend earned for her a debt of gratitude which can never be repaid. For days and nights did my sweet young nurse watch by my bed-side. I would take neither medicine nor suste-

nance, except from her hands. It is enough to say
that I recovered, and have since centered all the
affection of my heart on the gentle and tender being
to whom I owe my life. She, poor child, was
equally alone with myself. A father's love she had
never known, for Mr. Travers died when his only
child was an infant ; and his young widow, in a too
hasty second union forgot her duty towards her
first-born, and placed her exclusive affection on
the young progeny with which she was annually
blessing her second husband. The mother of Evelyn, being a woman of a very inferior order of
mind to her daughter, with the best intentions in
the world could never have duly appreciated her.
One very sore subject with the Dale family was the
knowledge that Evelyn must eventually inherit the
whole of her mother's jointure, in addition to her
own fortune, while the sole heritage of her half-
brothers and sisters would be the paternal debts,
which were considerable. All these circumstances
combined to induce the unloved girl to centre her
heart anywhere rather than on her nearest kindred ;
she felt that even school was more to her like home
than the house of her stepfather, and dreaded
the hour when she would be forced to leave the
shelter of its walls for so uncongenial a spot as
Warenne Vicarage. How often in the quiet noon,

or in the fragrant August evenings of our brief
autumn vacation, have we together paced the
gravelled path of the school garden, as I with
friendly counsels enforced by my four years' seni-
ority, endeavored to reconcile the weeping child to
her lot, to impress upon her mind the duty of seeking the flowers that grow by the pathway of life
rather than the thorns, with which they are ever in-
termingled. I must not, however, omit to describe
my heroine, whom I confess to have regarded with
eyes somewhat partial—for to me she was the type
of all that is most lovely in woman. Imagine,
then, features of such faultless regularity that except
in a statue, rarely, if ever, have I looked upon their
like—a complexion slightly tinged with brown, but
so transparent that the color deepened at every
movement, and varied with each passing word.
Pencilled brows, overarching long almond-shaped
eyes, whose predominant expression in repose was
one of pensive thoughtfulness, but which in moments of mirth, actually sparkled and danced with
fun, as the dimples of laughter broke over her
cheek, and the lips parted to show the pearls within.
Imagine, too, hair of the softest texture, and of that
peculiar shade of brown which looks bright in the
sunbeam, but dark in the shade, and a fairy figure
which if as yet somewhat too thin, gave full prom-

ise in after life, of ripening into the rounded perfection of maturity. Such is the portrait of Evelyn Travers, when in her sixteenth year she left school, and, accompanied by her faithful mentor, (as she would playfully term me) returned to the residence of her mother.

Warenne Vicarage was a fine old house, full of queer old gables, built in what is termed the Elizabethian style. It stood far back in its own grounds, which were parcelled out into flower garden, orchard, and vegetable garden—also there was a charming walk called "the glebe," a series of meadows sloping upward, bounded by a pleasant green path and a hedge fragrant with the sweetbrier - rose and eglantine. In this lover's walk, did we two friends pass many a long hour, weaving sweet fancies, as hope, that lovely but deceitful syren, lifted for us, with fairy wand, the curtain of futurity. Happy is it for us, that in youth, the far-off horizon ever appears to be bathed in sunshine! In the dawn of life we are like a rose, our illusions the leaves; these drop, one by one, as we bear the burden and heat of the day—and in the evening who would recognize that flower which looked so lovely, and yielded so sweet a perfume, when sprinkled with the dew of earliest morning? In truth, a little poesy was needed, to enable us to support our sur-

roundings with becoming philosophy. The Rev.
Mr. Dale, the Vicar, had in his younger days been
a military man, and even in the army had the reputation of being *fast*. Indeed, so fast had he been,
that it was as a ruined spendthrift that he addressed
the handsome, but imprudent young widow, who
later became his wife. We fear that in the eyes of
the admiring lover the lady's jointure was by no
means the least of her attractions. " *Veni, Vidi,
Vici*," was his watchword, and in less than six
weeks from the commencement of their acquaintance the happy pair entered into the bliss of the
honey-moon. Matrimony somewhat sobers a man.
The reckless spendthrift remembering the old adage,
" The greater the sinner the greater the saint," commenced studying divinity, with a view to entering
the church ; for, as his newly-made wife very justly
observed to her lord, "A nice parsonage would
save house-rent." In less than two years, therefore, Mr. and Mrs. Dale were installed in a small
house attached to a curacy.

As time passed onward the reverend gentleman
began to evince decided Low Church tendencies; the
reason of this became shortly apparent on his receiving from an evangelical elderly maiden lady in the
parish, the presentation to a very fat living, which
was intended as a provision for her Puseyite nephew,

who was by reason of his disappointment driven into the arms of the Church of Rome. From this moment the Vicar became quite a saint—in his own estimation at least—and to prove his "title to the skies" he condemned every one who did not share his theological opinions to the infernal regions.—Here let me make one observation, which is that although I have met many of all creeds, who devoutly believe in eternal punishment—*for their neighbors*—and who are quite annoyed if any presume to throw a doubt on this dogma of their several churches, I have never as yet met *one* who expected *himself* to be eternally lost, or who did not profess the hope of salvation he denied to others. Accordingly the Vicar asserted about seven times a day on an average, that *he* was *sure* of Heaven whatever he had done, or might yet do, because *Christ died for him.* This pernicious doctrine is, sad to say, frequently held by what in England is termed the Low Church or evangelical party, in contradistinction to the High Church and Puseyites, who are considered, especially the latter, to favor too much the Romish doctrine of the necessity of good works. All our neighbors, no matter how amiable or charitable, were pitilessly black-balled by Mr. Dale as children of the Evil One. Alas, that a minister of our Divine Master should so far forget that great precept, " Judge not

that ye be not judged." Alas! that he should thus ig-
nore the apostolic teachings and forget that " charity
thinketh no evil."   Our society was naturally much
restricted; two or three half-starved curates and a
few long-visaged ladies of " undoubted piety " were
alone permitted occasionally to taste of the hospitality of the Vicar. Hence too we were condemned to
be present at long family prayers, with scripture ex-
poundings, and nasal hymn-singing twice a day. A
lecture in church, a couple of prayer-meetings, and
another to consider prophecy, we were also expected
to attend every week in the cottage of some elect
brother or sister.

Evelyn, ever impetuous, almost took a disgust to
Religion held up to her example in so distasteful a
form. She was young and ardent, and her judgment was that of a child. " Oh, Mary !" she would
exclaim, " CAN Heaven be made up of such people?
—if so, surely, surely it will not be a very pleasant
place."   In after years my readers will perceive
that the sentiments of my by no means faultless heroine were greatly modified on many subjects.

Thus passed the summer and autumn. I had arranged (by the payment of a small annual sum) to
make my friend's home my own. I confess to entertaining the hope, that Evelyn, surrounded by
such uncongenial spirits, would remain unmarried

at least four or five years, when, in my girlish ideas, I considered we should, or certainly I should, be very old, and sufficiently steady, having joined our incomes, to fly away together to sunny Italy. It was, however, otherwise ordained.

CHAPTER II.

COURTSHIP.

ONE morning at breakfast, on opening the letter-bag, Mrs. Dale announced to her husband that her nephew, Captain Travers, of the *** Lancers, had just returned from India, and proposed paying them a visit at Christmas. Had the Vicar been a devout Catholic, he would doubtless have crossed himself, as it was he gave a kind of holy groan, and rolled up his forehead, as he was wont to do when any very obstinate sinner was mentioned. The lady, however, pressed her point, and at length a reluctant consent was given, together with the expression of a despairing hope that the visit of this probable child of Satan might eventually " be blessed " to the saving of his soul. Mrs. Dale, whose piety was by no means so lively as that of her husband, was only too happy to have an occasion for arraying herself in some of the elegant new dresses she had surreptitiously procured at the nearest town. She therefore lost no time in answering the gallant captain by letter that they would be delighted to welcome him to Warenne Vicarage. I perceived that Evelyn was much preoccupied by her cousin's projected visit; our life was so monotonous that any change was welcome, and a young and dashing officer of cavalry could not fail to be an acquisition to our very limited and somewhat dull clerical circle. Frequently I interrupted her day dreams, begging her not to imagine she was about to meet her " beau ideal "— the hero of her young imaginings—or she would surely be disappointed. With a bright blush she would reply, " You know, dear Mary, how high is my standard of perfection, and that I hope never to marry unless I meet one I can not only love, but respect and revere above all created beings. Yet," she added with a sigh, " how in this isolated spot may I ever hope to meet with such a man? unless indeed," smiling archly, " my gallant cousin prove to be my own true knight," and springing lightly across the room to her harp, she would commence singing, in a rich contralto voice, Mrs. Norton's exquisite ballad, " Love not, ye hapless sons of clay," or perhaps one of Moores' delicious national airs.— She was one of the few gifted individuals who have " tears in the voice," so deep was the pathos, so intense the feeling, she threw into both words and

melody; like Orpheus, she might have charmed even
the rocks. Thus passed the days till Christmas time
drew nigh, with its promise of turkeys, roast beef,
mince pies and plum puddings. Mrs. Dale "on
household thoughts intent," spent many an hour in
superintending the preparation of mince meat, sau-
sages, and other delicacies, for country folks make
all these luxuries at home. Of course your humble
servant was pressed into the service, but our heroine, who detested the details of the "ménage," (for
which she was always and with reason scolded by
her mother), continued to practice her harp and her
singing, and to write her foolish, romantic thoughts
in her journal, utterly heedless of all sublunary mat-
ters, and alike inattentive to the maternal reproofs
and to the more gentle remonstrances of her Mentor. At length the long-expected and anxiously desired day dawned bleak and cheerless in appearance,
but fraught with sunshine to the now cheerful party
at the Vicarage. Our usual two o'clock dinner was
postponed to the hour of half-past five to suit the
more aristocratic habits of the young officer. Even
Mr. Dale fetched from the cellar a bottle of his oldest port, and the whole house wore an air of unacus-
tomed festivity. Precisely at half-past four, the
roll of a carriage and a loud ring at the door-bell,
announced the much desired arrival. The usual

kindly greetings over, the visitor was ushered to the guest-chamber. I had just completed my toilet, and wishing to ascertain if Evelyn had done the same, entered her apartment. I was quite struck by her extreme beauty. She was robed in an exquisitely-fitting dinner costume of blue silk, which suited well with her delicate features and bright but soft complexion. A scarf of white tulle was gracefully flung around her shoulders, I may add, in the words of Byron,

> " Her glossy hair was braided o'er a brow
> Bright with intelligence—"

And one camelia from the green-house, of the softest pink, reposed on her rich and wavy tresses. I do not think that Evelyn was then aware how very lovely she was, and this unconsciousness of effect greatly enhanced her charms. " How nice you look, dear Mary," were her words, as she placed her arm within mine and we descended to the drawing-room. Mrs. Dale was already there, looking very handsome in a dress of black satin, her dark hair in short curls under a pretty cap of blond and flowers. She was still a remarkably fine woman, and had she been less stout, would by no means have looked her age. A few moments and our newly arrived guest entered, ushered in by the Vicar. Captain

Edward Travers was a young man of gentleman-like manners and prepossessing appearance. He was dressed in the height of fashion, which in England means a well-cut coat, white waist-coat, an irreproachable neck-tie, and well-fitting polished boots. As the captain shook hands with us, his smile displayed a fine set of teeth—his eyes likewise were good, and altogether, my first impressions respecting him were agreeable. An evangelical curate completed the party, and to Evelyn's horror took her in to dinner—the principal guest, of course, being seated at the right hand of the lady of the house. Dinner passed off; and shortly after the removal of the cloth the ladies retired, and the gentlemen remained to finish their wine—a remnant to my mind of the barbarous ages.

In the evening, Evelyn and myself played duetts on the harp and piano. She also sang to my accompaniment various pretty ballads, both English and German. Meanwhile Captain Travers talked much—too much, I thought, during the music—to Mrs. Dale; and at ten precisely the entrance of the servants for family prayers put an end for that day to our occupations.

On retiring, Evelyn sought my room. "Well, Mary," said she, "what think you of my cousin?"

"He appears pleasant and good natured," said I. "And you?"

"Oh! all I know is, that you need not imagine I have found my ideal knight."

"He is, however, good looking?"

"Yes—has fine eyes."

"Yes—and above all," I added, laughing, "a most becoming moustache."

"Oh! decidedly—I confess to a weakness for moustache; one may then be quite sure the man is no curate—eh! Mary?—But he talks too much, and evidently cares not for music."

- Like a couple of school-girls, we continued to chatter till near midnight, when, declaring I was half asleep, I playfully ejected the young lady by main force from my room, and was soon in the land of dreams.

A week passed, and our guest was to leave on the morrow. I had ceased to think about him, except as one of those common-place individuals, of whom the best description is, that "there is nothing in him." He appeared much pleased with the society of his aunt, seeming greatly to prefer it to that of his cousin. I was therefore surprised, the last evening, to see him bending over Evelyn's harp, and addressing her for some time in a low voice. I soon concluded he was explaining to her

some of the delights of the hunting-field, or, perhaps, expatiating on the scarcity of game this sea-
s n, and paid no further attention to them.
Judge, then, how utterly amazed I was, to learn
from Evelyn, that her cousin had proposed, and
that she had not positively rejected him.

"Good heavens!" I exclaimed, "you have not
been half so foolish! No—I will not believe it;
there must be some mistake. Repeat me the conversation, dear Evelyn."

"Perhaps, Mary, you will smile at the originality
of the affair. After many words about nothing, and
'a propos' to less, he suddenly said, 'I think I
shall sell out, and go abroad. Will you consent to
come with me, and make me happy?' Imagine my
surprise.—What could I say, except that I did not
know him sufficiently well, and that I would speak
to my mother—always having understood that is
the manner in which young ladies reply to pro-
posals, unless they are really in love—which, of
course, Mary, I am not. Now you know all that
has passed. I shall, after consulting mama, make
my definite decision; to-morrow, probably, will
decide my fate."

She left me, and I passed a sleepless night; for I
perceived no promise of happiness for her, in so
hasty an engagement. I sincerely trusted her mo-

ther would dissuade her from committing so sad a folly, and anxiously awaited the events of the coming day.

After breakfast, I saw poor Evelyn led into the drawing-room, like a lamb to the slaughter, by her mother, and left alone with the young man. Suspense was becoming unbearable, when, after about an hour had elapsed, Evelyn flew to my room, and flung herself into my arms:

"Oh, dearest," she said, sobbing, "my only true friend, let me confide in you. Last night I went, as you know, to mama's room, and told her all, adding that I did not love him, and felt no inclination to marry. She chid me, saying I ought to consider myself fortunate—that she could not imagine *why* I did not love so charming a young fellow, and adding, that 'love *before* marriage was quite unnecessary, as every well brought up girl was sure to love her husband when once she had become a wife.' My mother concluded by saying that if I were so silly as not to accept my cousin, she would take no further trouble to introduce me into society, and that I must make up my mind to live here all my life. So you see, Mary, I was in a measure forced to say, that if on further acquaintance, I could like him, I would be his wife."

"My poor darling," said I, smoothing her soft

hair, " better bear your present troubles than blind-
ly rush into, perhaps, far greater sorrow."

"Mary," replied Evelyn, "do not think me childish, but I cannot endure this methodistical house.
Besides, I long to see the world—to go to balls,
the opera, theatres. Better to be really unhappy
than die of *ennui*. The stormiest sea is surely superior to a stagnant pool. Besides, he is really
fond of me. You should have seen how his hand
trembled."

I ventured to interrupt her here, and to suggest
that the hand occasionally shook at breakfast, also,
when there was no apparent cause.

" For shame, Mary," she said, (though I do not
think she then understood my fears,) "indeed I feel
certain he adores me. I shall be petted, and spoiled ;
I will do my duty, and try to make him happy.
Oh ! I will be a model wife."

Tears had already given place to smiles and dimples, on the face of my sweet friend, and the hope
of a happier future had brought light to her eyes,
and renewed bloom to her cheek. I could not find
it in my heart to dash her joy, so I twined my arms
around her, reiterating my fervent wishes for her
happiness, and adding, that whether for weal or woe,
she would ever find a firm friend, and a loving sister,
in Mary Mildmay.

CHAPTER III.

In order that our readers may comprehend the motives by which some of the actors in this our drama of real life were actuated, we must cast a retrospective glance at the past and view our heroine in her infancy, as the only and beloved child of a doting father. Mr. Travers married late in life a pretty, penniless girl, and found himself in failing health with a young wife and infant daughter to provide for. Had this child been a son, he would have been heir to landed estates entailed in the male line, but to a girl Mr. Travers could only leave a sum of money he possessed in the funds, and of this, he settled the half on his widow for life with reversion to Evelyn at her mother's death; the remainder was left as a marriage portion to the former, or, if unmarried, she was to come into the full control of her property on attaining the age of eighteen, Mrs. Travers acting as sole guardian of her daughter. A codicil to the will, with pardonable family pride, expressed the wish that Evelyn might marry the son of the testator's half brother, Edward, who must eventually become the possessor of the whole entailed family property. Thus having, as he thought, secured the welfare and happiness of his unconscious babe, the noble father and loyal husband was called to a better and a happier world, where we trust he may hereafter hold sweet communion with his child when the trials and troubles of her mortal life shall be at an end.

Let us now return to our present hero and the lady of his dreams. In consequence of the state of affairs Captain Edward Travers prolonged his stay at the Vicarage another ten days, during which time the youthful pair took daily walks about the grounds we have already described. In the evening they sat indefatigably together, and to judge by the absence of conversation when in the house, I should say they must have exhausted all topics of interest during their morning strolls, for they literally appeared to have nothing to say to each other. I confess to quite a feeling of relief, as I watched the phaeton drive through the large front gates of the Vicarage, *en route* for the railway station, bearing the young officer away. I hoped that absence would *not* in this case, " make the heart grow fonder," but

that Evelyn would permit her better judgment
to influence her, and perceive she was on the
eve of committing an irretrievable folly. I
was confirmed in this opinion, on observing the
blank look of surprise, even mortification, on
her mobile countenance, as she perused her first
love letter, an event usually so delightful to a young
girl, and then, without a word, placed the interesting missive in the hands of her mother. That lady,
it appeared, was decidedly a friend to the absent.
She glanced over the letter, exclaiming, as she read
it :—

"Dear fellow; how he loves you, Evelyn. See
how his hand trembled from excitement; the writing is almost illegible."

And so, in very truth, was it, and horribly ill-
spelled, if that too, be a symptom of the tender passion. The letter, however, commenced, "My darling Evelyn," and ended, "Yours for life."

Now, let me ask you young ladies of sweet six-
teen, would not your pretty little heads have been
slightly turned, if you had for the first time in your
lives, been thus addressed by a good-looking, rich
young officer, with real moustaches? And this too,
even though the orthography of the epistle might
have been somewhat defective. My heroine, though
full of intelligence, somewhat lacked that invaluable

quality—plain, common sense. Nor was she in any way above the faults and weaknesses of her age and sex. Let not my readers then be surprised if she permitted her own charity, and the writer's evident attachment, to " cover a multitude of (*grammatical*) sins." One thing was self-evident from the tone of the gallant captain's correspondence, namely : that he considered Evelyn as his *fiancée*, and wrote as an accepted suitor.

The letter was duly answered, and shortly after another made its appearance, which, to judge by its defective style, argued no diminution of the tender passion, for the lover's head and hand evidently partook of the agitated state of his heart, always interpreting these signs as favorably as did our lovely heroine and her amiable mother. On handing the second of these interesting documents to his stepdaughter, the Rev. Mr. Dale expressed the wish for a few moments' conversation with her in his study. So, immediately, after breakfast we bent our steps thither, for Evelyn, who dreaded above all things a *tête-à-tête* with the Vicar, had insisted on my accompanying her.

I was with some difficulty admitted into the sanctum. We seated ourselves and prepared for a sermon. Meanwhile I was secretly rejoicing in the idea that the captain's attentions would surely be put an end to, on the plea of his being one of the "children of this world."

"My dear Evelyn," solemnly began the reverend gentleman, "I wish to know your exact position as regards your cousin."

"I thought, sir, mama had informed you."

"Yes, my dear, your mother mentioned to me very properly, that Travers had asked your hand, but she also added that no definite reply had been given to the young man. Has anything since occurred to alter your sentiments?"

"No sir; they are the same as before, or, rather, perhaps I ought to say"—turning very red and trembling visibly—"I—I——"

"Well, child," said the Vicar, smiling, "you like him rather better, eh?"

"Oh, no sir," said poor Evelyn, almost in tears. "Since I have read his letters I fear—indeed—I—"

"Evelyn," said Mr. Dale, severely, "I am surprised at your conduct; you have gone farther than a modest girl ought, with any man who is not to be her husband. Your reputation—if you do not now marry—is lost. You will acquire the name of flirt and jilt, and no honorable man will ever again look at you."

"But, sir, how could I know whether I should like him?"

" I tell you, young lady," said her stepfather, " as
one who knows the world, and can speak with authority, " you have been seen too much together,
and I will add, that as in your unconverted state,
you could never hope to marry a Christian, you
should consider yourself *most fortunate* in having
attached to you so amiable a worldling. Now, say
no more, foolish child," (kissing her brow with
some show of affection. " Go to your mother, talk
all this over with her, and may God bless you."

We were leaving the room, when Mr. Dale called
Evelyn back, and I heard him tell her, that she
must, now that she was going to be married, prepare also to become a woman of business; adding, " but your mother will explain all "— then,
in a louder voice, " Mind, child, *I* have nothing to
do with it."

Evelyn joined Mrs. Dale, who usually sat work-
ing in her morning room. The result of their con-
ference (to which I was not admitted,) was, that a
letter was dispatched from his future *belle mère*,
to Captain Travers, giving her formal consent to his
projected union with her daughter; and, two days
later, I was sent to Paris, on a visit to the dear old
school, with full and ample instructions as to the
Corbeille de mariage, which the fair *fiancée* was
to provide for herself. Nor was the little busi-

ness affair alluded to by the Rev. Mr. Dale forgotten. A letter of instructions was written by Evelyn, under her mother's dictation, to her solicitors, Messrs. Takeall & Co., the result of which was highly advantageous to the reverend gentleman.

Let us charitably hope, that in thus sacrificing a young, beautiful, and talented daughter, to a man she did not love, Mrs. Dale was in a measure actuated by her desire to fulfil the dying wish of Evelyn's father. We fear, however, that another less praiseworthy motive had some influence on her decision.

By no means so saint-like as her spouse, this lady had a great hankering after forbidden pleasure, and she doubtless thought in her inmost heart, that a yearly visit to a gay and worldly house, she might, in fact, term her second home, would be a most agreeable change from the rather monotonous society of the elect. If such were her idea, she was doomed to disappointment.

Early in the morning of the eventful day, Evelyn was summoned to the sitting room of her mother. She was there introduced to the very respectable legal adviser of the family, Mr. Takeall, a gentleman of some fifty summers, with a pair of uncomfortable, restless eyes, whose expression was somewhat concealed by a pair of spectacles.

2*

"Well, well, young lady," said the man of law, very blandly; "so we are going to be married, are we?—and we wish to be quite a woman of business, do we? That's right—that's right. Now, here's just a *little* paper, to which we must put our name —of course, with mama's sanction—quite so?" looking at Mrs. Dale, who made a signal in the affirmative.

The worthy attorney then proceeded to business. He emptied his large blue bag of various parchments, sealed with large red seals, and tied with red tape. Among these, (as I afterwards learned,) was a deed by which Evelyn signed away in favor of her stepfather and his children, her interest in the reversion of her mother's fortune. This small sum of £15,000 had long been coveted by the Vicar. The manner of obtaining it, worldlings would be apt to call swindling; the reverend gentleman, probably, termed it, "ministering to the necessities of the saints." Be this as it may, it was none the less an illegal transaction, and caused, eventually, a complete break between the Travers and Dale families.

The signatures duly affixed, the wily attorney took hold of both the young girl's hands. "And now, my fair client," said he, "you have been generous—very generous—a good daughter, very. Allow me, my good young lady, to wish you every

happiness; and pray remember, Messrs. Takeall &
Co. will be only too happy to serve you in any way
in their power."

"Thank you, sir," replied the poor victim, struggling to free her hands, which the bland lawyer
kept shaking; "but you forget that a bride must
dress."

"Quite so—quite so," said Mr. Takeall, releasing
her. And as she left the room, he continued, in his
most caressing tones, "That's a good girl, my dear
Mrs. Dale—"a *very* good girl. You have reason to
be proud of your daughter, madam—quite so, quite
so," as he rolled up parchments and papers, and
stowed them away in his capacious bag.

CHAPTER IV.

THE BRIDAL.

THOUGH the morning of the wedding had dawned serene and cloudless, the glare of the treacherous sun of May, was accompanied by the cutting east wind, so prevalent in England in that month—fit emblem of the chequered course of married life, the transient joys of which are but too apt to wither beneath the chill breezes of disappointment. My young lady readers, *never marry in May*—that reputed most unlucky month for hymeneal ceremonies. As far as my experience goes, I have invariably seen this popular superstition verified by the result.

The wedding of the two cousins was quiet and private, the guests invited being restricted to the immediate relatives and connexions of the young couple. The bride, who was in high beauty, wore over a petticoat of white glacé silk a richly-embroidered robe of India muslin, the gift of her husband, who had brought it from India. Her wreath and bou-

quet were of real orange flowers and myrtle, and a
veil of the most delicate lace enveloped her youthful form, as in a cloud. Her two young sisters, a
friend and myself, in white tarletan, trimmed with
pink, and looking like rose-buds around a queenly
white moss-rose, formed the bridal train; and six
little girls from the Sunday school, dressed in white,
strewed flowers in their beloved teacher's path.
Evelyn, "the observed of all observers," did not, I
think, appear fully to realize the solemnity of the
occasion, though I fancied I perceived a slight shudder pass through her frame, as the irrevocable words
were uttered, which fixed her destiny forever. I,
for my part, could not shake off a certain gloom, by
no means appropriate to so festive an occasion; but
I tried hard to be cheerful: and it was not until
the last farewells were spoken, and Evelyn smiling,
but tearful, was seated in her britschka, by the side
of her good-looking young husband, that I sought
the solitude of my chamber, and gave full and un-
restrained vent to my feelings.

Evelyn's first letters, though short, were happy
and hopeful. She made a tour of about six weeks
in the northern counties of England, visiting also a
part of Scotland.

Soon after her return to the house of her husband, which, my readers will remember, was also

that of her beloved, though unknown father, I received from my friend a long letter, which I shall proceed to transcribe, that she may speak for herself:

EVELYN TRAVERS TO MARY MILDMAY.

The Abbey, Woodlands, Derbyshire,
July ——, 18——.

You upbraid me for my long silence and short letters, my own Mary, forgetting that I have been, for the last few weeks, incessantly on the move, besides having suffered, with becoming patience, that infliction miscalled "the honey-moon," which, with the exception of courtship, is certainly the dullest and most unprofitable period of one's life. Now that I am settled in my new home, or rather, shall I not say, in my beloved *old* home, (for was it not that of my father?) I can sit down and endeavor to fulfil your wishes, by giving you a detailed account of all you may desire to know.

First, then, this is the dearest old place in the world—inexpressibly so to me, for the sake of that dear father, whom, though unknown, I love better than any living thing. Even as I write, I have his full-length portrait before me—of life-size, and so like my impression of him, that I should have recognized it anywhere. Yes, there are the mild blue eyes, the noble features, the intellectual brow, I have frequently seen bending over my conch in my dreams, when I felt happy—*so* happy in the thought that, though absent in body, he might, perhaps, still be permitted, by a mysterious Providence, to guide and guard his daughter. My husband and myself have an apartment in the left wing of the old Abbey, which is completely overgrown with ivy. We have a bed-chamber, with two dressing-rooms attached—a smoking cabinet for Edward, full of guns, and ugly-looking hooks to torment the poor fishes; and worse than all—I regret to say—the chimney is ornamented with hideous old pipes, of all shapes and sizes. There is, of course, a drawing room, and the sweetest boudoir for me. This completes our suite of apartments. Stay—I am wrong. There is yet another room, with hangings of blue and white, (your favorite colors) which I have already named, Mary's " Canserie," in the fond hope it will shortly be occupied by her. Am I wrong? My boudoir is quite a "ladye's bower," its latticed windows, overlooking the flower-garden, include also a more distant view of the park, with a glimpse of the blue hills of Derbyshire, the lordly Peak towering far above his companions in the dim and distant horizon. Our beautiful Woodlands well deserves its name; the Park is rich in its old ances-

tral trees, and abounds in grassy knolls ; and a river, sparkling and clear as crystal, filled with trout,
meanders through the grounds, preserving the
freshness and enhancing the beauty of the scene.

Fortunate creature, I think I hear you exclaim,
and truly, I can imagine no happier lot than to
have called such a place by the sweet name of
home in my girlhood.

But, alas ! as it is, I envy the deer, the birds, the
flowers, their freedom. Oh, Mary ! when starting on my first journey as a wife, you placed in
my hands a volume of Byron, your parting remembrance, you little thought what a fatal gift it would
prove to me. It has opened a new field of romance,
and from a child your poor Evelyn has sprung into
womanhood. I now know the kind feeling I bear
towards my husband is not worthy the name of
love. How then could I continue to deceive him
by permitting him to believe the contrary ? No ; I
thought it my duty to confess to him that I never
did, and never could love him. And he—loves me
better than his dog, and a little less than his horse.

What a prospect, when one is not yet seventeen !
You will tell me no one is to blame but myself.
I deny this. I am the creature of circumstance,
and could not have done otherwise than I have done.
But to return to our family circle. You saw my

father-in-law at the wedding; a good-hearted, frank,
generous, but somewhat rough, country squire, who
makes a great pet of his new daughter. His wife,
a tall, lanky, uninteresting lady, with stony eyes,
who studies nothing but her own health, fancying
herself a confirmed invalid. She lives almost entirely
in her own apartments, only occasionally appear-
ing at dinner, to which she does, however, most ample justice. This is the only time she ever sees the
good squire, her husband, and even then she is bare-
ly civil to him. Not a very good example for us
young people. Both parents dote on their only son,
and each appears jealous of the other's influence
over him. My father-in-law, with Edward, sometimes sit too long over their wine, usually, indeed,
not making their appearance in the drawing-room
till it is almost time to think of retiring for the
night, and then they throw themselves into an arm
chair or on a sofa and fall asleep. It is not, as you
may suppose, very amusing for me, and only makes
me pine the more for your society. Do you remember, Mary, how you used to tease me and tell
me I was not going to marry a man, " but a pair of
moustaches?" Well, I confess, they may have had
a trifle to do with it, but only just imagine my horror: Edward appeared yesterday morning at breakfast shorn of his honors, and on my my exclamation

of natural disgust, he informed me that his name having appeared in the gazette as having sold out of the army, he was no longer entitled as a civilian, to wear moustaches. I never thought my husband *clever*, I knew he did not care for music, nor understand poetry, but I *did* fancy him good-looking, and now, Mary, the worst is to come—I actually think him ugly—his long upper-lip, robbed of its greatest ornament, has such a sullen, almost sulky expression, when he is serious or asleep, that I actually shudder when I look at him. You who are so sensible, and so *posée*— excuse a most expressive French word—will perhaps not understand this, and will certainly blame me, and yet all these feelings are involuntary. And now, dear Mary, hasten here to your foolish, unhappy, childish, but certainly loving, friend, who will count the weary hours till she can welcome you to her new home.

Your attached
EVELYN.

CHAPTER V.

THE country homes of old England, standing amid their ancestral trees, what visions of quiet happiness do they recall to my mind! Memory loves to linger before thy hospitable portal, oh, Rookwood! and hear once more the kindly greeting of the amiable and affectionate family, some of whose members, alas! now sleep their last sleep—the others are dead, at least to me; for

> " The absent are the dead, for they are cold,
> And ne'er can we what once we did behold;
> And they are changed—"

Far more so, than the departed, who ever watch us with their loving eyes, changeless, immortal.

A verdant spot in life's desert was that dear home to me, whose halls ever resounded with the cheerful laughter of its happy and beloved in-

mates — the sisters all that women ought to
be — the brothers, noble, manly, and gallant
as the knights of old—the venerable father, indulgent, yet firm as a rock—the mother, whom
I never knew, excepting by her portrait, a lovely countenance, gentle and tender as a Madonna
of Raphael.

Each nook and dell of that fair Park is engraven
on my heart of hearts. On this grassy slope, I
walked with Mary, as she bent her steps toward
the village, where the poor awaited her with bless-
ings. In yonder pleasant path, Anne, the wit of the
family, almost killed me with laughter. On that
gently-rising eminence, the hounds threw off—and
there, after a hard day's run, William, the eldest son,
who was ever in at the death, presented my delighted self with the brush. Under the shade of
those wavy beeches, which every moment strewed
their leaves in our path, did the graceful and chivalrous George teach the timid school-girl to ride, or
rather, to manage her rein ; he was a very Bayard
on horseback, and a kind horse-master to boot. He
loved to see the noble animals well and judiciously
treated, whether on the road or in the stable. I remember a saying he had, which amused us all
immensely—it was this :

"Never 'ammer your 'unter along a 'ard road—
if you wish to 'ammer along a 'ard road, 'ire a 'ack
and 'ammer 'im."

George was handsome, accomplished, and good—
to my girlish fancy, a very "*preux chevalier, sans
peur et sans reproche*"—but he was a decided
lady's man, and, of course, a passionate and rather
general admirer of beauty. I knew I was not handsome, so I never again accepted an invitation to
join that dear and happy circle; and thus ended the
one romance of my life.

But this is a digression. My readers will remember the very pressing invitation I had received from
Mrs. Edward Travers, to join her at Woodlands;
nevertheless, I judged it unadvisable, for the present, to accede to her wishes, trusting that, thrown
entirely on her husband for society, the young wife
might, in time, learn to consider him as her first and
best friend. It was, therefore, not until the first
week in October, that I started from Warenne
Vicarage, at about 7 A. M., for the railway station,
in order to take the train, which met the express
from London, as this was the only one which would
enable me to reach Woodlands the same evening.

It was one of those lovely and soft, yet fresh
mornings peculiar to our climate, at this season of
the year, when the sky, though serene, is not cloud

less, and the air is at the same time balmy and
exhilarating, and, as it were, charged with vitality.
The white hoar frost clung like gems to the blades
of grass, and caused the varied tints of the Autumn
leaves to appear still more fresh and glowing.

I, for my part, confess to feeling great delight in
railway travelling—the commencement of a journey, especially if the end of it promises pleasure,
always raises my spirits in fine weather.

In England, this mode of locomotion is more than
comfortable—it is luxurious. The termini and the
stations are so well ordered, that you may obtain
your ticket at your ease, without that rushing and
pushing incident to all other European countries.
If you have to wait the train, you do so in a clean
and comfortable room in winter with a large fire;
or, if a lady, you can remain in an inner room, with
dressing-room attached, where you may command
the services of a female attendant. The first class
waiting rooms are, of course, much better than
those of the second and third classes, though these
also have every reasonable convenience. Should
the carriages be in waiting at the terminus, (which
is usually the case) the traveller, after securing his
ticket, may instantly take his place, and, arrang-
ing his dressing-case, wraps, &c., comfortably
ensconce himself in his seat, before the arrival of

the less punctual passengers. If our traveller have taken a first-class ticket, he will find, even if he has filled a second place with his necessary encumbrances, he will rarely be disturbed; for those who in England can afford to pay for the best accommodations, are usually of a class to whom good manners are habitual—they will, therefore, rather seek another seat than put a fellow-passenger to inconvenience. The railway companies being most liberal with their carriages, the chances are, if you arrive early and manage well, you will always secure room for your legs. Six places are the usual complement of each first-class compartment; these have elastic cushions, and are partitioned off with arms, like an easy-chair, so as to allow the occupant of each seat to lean back. The French arrangements are still more commodious— while the German second class, " Wagen," is equal in comfort to the English and French first class carriages. These latter, in Germany, are literally small " salons," containing a sofa, arm-chairs, centre-table, and even large and handsome mirrors on the walls.

What a contrast to the American cars! Surely, Madame de Stael must have had prophetic vision of these odious vehicles, when she declared travelling to be " *Le plus triste plaisir de la vie*"—for I can testify, that the old *diligence*, with its numerous inconveniences, is as the gates of Paradise, compared to the straight-backed benches of cotton velvet, the stuffy atmosphere, and the miscellaneous and unsavory company in a Yankee car! The *coupé* of a diligence, at least, permits of cleanliness and privacy; but where, Oh! ye Goths and Vandals, may we take refuge, in this land of "liberty and equality"—but *not* "fraternity"—from squalling babies, tobacco-juice, spittoons, and the great unwashed?

My readers, even though Americans, must pardon these observations. There are very many fine institutions in this splendid country; but there is also much room for improvement.

The American steamboats can "whip all others out of creation;" but land travelling leaves much to be desired. All these thoughts might posssibly have passed through the writer's mind, had she been an American, as she flew, with the speed of the wind, through the green and highly-cultivated meadows of Merry England, seated in the luxurious *fauteuil* of a first-class carriage.

The journey was without incident or accident. On reaching the Derby-junction station, the train for that Shire, was, in railway phrase, "shunted" on to the midland-counties line. A sandwich and a cup of coffee, hastily swallowed, and away flew the train, at the speed of sixty miles an hour, through a rich country, diversified by hill, wood, and water— all glowing in the beams of the now setting sun. One hour more, and we stop. I catch a glimpse of the most coquettish little hat in the world, shading a radiant and lovely young face. Springing out, I am caught and kissed, and hurried into a carriage in waiting. One moment, and John, the footman, touching his hat, says: " Please, ma'am, the luggage is all right." A pretty, silvery voice at my side, replies: " Very well—home." John mounts the box, and Evelyn and myself are once more together and alone.

CHAPTER VI

HOME SCENES.

Evelyn's home was comfortable without being luxurious, and well suited to a family of moderate fortune. Charmingly situate, in the loveliest of England's midland counties, the house, originally an old monastery, stood in the midst of a richly wooded though not very extensive park. The amusements at Woodlands, as is the case more or less all over England, were more suitable to gentlemen than to the fairer sex. They consisted, principally, of hunting, shooting, and fishing in some of the trout streams hard by. The Squire, as he was usually termed, with his son, Captain Travers, constantly availed themselves of these facilities for sport; consequently we ladies were left almost entirely on our own resources. An occasional dinner party, to which we were expected to drive out some ten or twelve miles, in full evening costume, perhaps on a snowy night, formed the only variety to our rather monotonous life. These dinner parties were altogether "flat, stale and unprofitable." The usual codfish, with oyster sauce, saddle of mutton, and boiled chicken or turkey, were served up, and flavored by such conversation as the following:

"A fine day for scent, eh, Squire?"

"Glorious; were you in at the death?"

"I should say so. By Jove! my mare's a clipper, I can tell you."

"Smith, your grey rather swerved at that fence."

"Why, yes; my fool of a groom physicked him only a week since, and the fence was a stiff-un, but he's a very devil to go."

Or thus:

"I say, gov'n'r," (the s.ang term for father,) "how many birds d'ye say we bagged to-day?"

"Well, fifteen brace."

"No, twenty, I tell ye, all fine uns."

"That dog of yours, Travers, is a capital setter, and no mistake. What's his pedigree?"

"Oh, he was got by Tommy out of Fairstar."

"I should like a pup of his, by Jove!"

After dinner, on the adjournment of the ladies to the drawing-room, the sporting talk commences in right earnest, the wine circulating even more briskly than before. The married ladies meanwhile stand around a roaring fire warming their satin-clad feet;

they complain to each other of the delinquencies of
their servants, or boast of the beauty and precocity
of their children. The entrance, presently, of coffee,
puts an end to general conversation, as the ladies collect into smaller groups to wait for tea and the gentlemen. The matrons and elderly maidens perhaps
indulge in a little scandal as they sip the fragrant
beverage. The more juvenile damsels talk of balls,
past and future, and of the delightful partners who
may have fallen to their lot. Some would be Grisi,
" inglorious," though not, alas! " mute," possibly at-
tacks the open piano with a violence that makes you
almost imagine she is venting her spite upon the
innocent instrument, and then in a cracked but sten-
torian voice, she commences to shout, " Sing me the
songs that to me were so dear, long, LONG ago, long,
LONG ago," accentuating the dashed expletives by a
shriller scream even than before. At about half-
past ten enter the lords of the creation, with highly
flushed faces, and vociferating loudly, the words,
" my good fellow," " horse," " dog," " my mare,"
" that pointer," still forming the burden of their
song. Very slight attention falls to the share of
the ladies. A young curate, perhaps, stands beside
the piano, turning the leaves of the music-book for
the squalling songstress. A whist table is frequently formed, but at eleven a move is made, and by

half-past, the carriage of the last guest has usually rolled from the door.

The cause of Captain Travers' shaking hand was now but too apparrent. The captain, I regret to say, seldom, if ever, returned home from these dinners perfectly sober, and the old squire, though rejoicing in a stronger head than his son, was but too often more than "a little elevated." Latterly the propensity of young Edward Travers became so uncontrollable that no invitations ever came from the best houses in the neighborhood to Woodlands, a very great slight to one of the oldest families in the county.

Our readers may readily imagine that though blessed with every outward advantage of person and position, our heroine felt more alone even than when cloistered within the walls of Warrenne Vicarage. Then at least she might hope for a brighter future ; now to hope were a crime, for would it not involve the death of another, and that other a husband. The marriage tie, in its spiritual and inner sense, is, indeed, as we are taught to believe, an inheritance from Paradise ; it supposes the perfect union of the sexes, so that two separate existences become virtually one individual. Neither would be complete without the other. Force blends with weakness ; firmness with gentleness ; and mutual

love and confidence is the crowning bliss of all.—
But observe the reverse of the picture, alas! far
more common than the other side. The hourly clash
of angry tempers and selfish desires, brutality and
neglect on the part of the husband, met by reproach-
es from the wife, and yet with all this, and perhaps
the vice of intoxication in addition, the wretched
pair must drag out a miserable existence till "death
do them part." Happy those countries where di-
vorce is permitted for other, though not slighter
causes than infidelity!

I mentioned that Evelyn, as a girl, was scarcely
aware either of her beauty or of her extreme power
of fascination. Now that she had become a married
child, older women spoiled her, telling her she had
thrown herself away, and that with advantages of
person and fortune such as hers, she might have aspired to become a duchess, or, as Evelyn added
with a sigh, "I might, had I waited, have met with
one worthy of my love, and have become a happy,
instead of an unloving and therefore wretched wife."
Often have I contrasted Rookwood—beloved home
of the intelligent, the refined, the sympathetic—
with the scarcely less beautiful Woodlands, the
abode of uncongenial spirits.

"Trifles," says a modern female writer,* "make

* Mrs. Hannah More.

the sum of human things;" and *she was right.* Happiness depends more on the hourly nothings of existence than we are fain to believe, and a continual dripping of water will wear away the hardest rock. The great sorrows of life are rare ; its intense joys rarer still; we have it in our power to embitter our own lot and that of others, or to be to them as a ministering angel and thus bring a blessing on ourselves. Did the young wife prepare to buy a a new dress, her husband would term it useless extravagance, and refuse to furnish her with the means for procuring it, even though these were actually of her own money. When she wished for a drive, the horses were required to go to cover, or they had a cough, or were in physic. Did Evelyn in the evening place herself at her harp, and sing in her sweetest and most thrilling tones, some of Moore's plaintive melodies, or of Mrs. Hemans' beautiful songs, the "thank you, my dear," of the kind but unappreciative Squire, would be echoed by a loud snore from his sleeping son, just in the most effective part of the performance. Later, when her health became delicate, as the prospect of maternity dawned upon her, even the visits of a physician in an "illness common to all women," as the Captain amiably remarked, were an unnecessary expense. Let not my readers imagine this was

"malice prepense"—it was only *selfishness*—that
bane of married life.

Edward Travers was the only son of foolish parents. His mother, selfish herself, and inconsiderate as to consequences, fostered his youthful vices;
and even on the rare occasions when the father
thought it necessary to correct his boy, the silly
and ill-tempered wife ever took the son's part
against the husband she so much disliked, and endeavored to compensate, by a larger slice of cake
or an extra glass of wine, that which she did not
scruple to impress on the lad's mind as unjustifiable
harshness on the part of the governor. Thus
trained up "in the way he should" not "go," can
it be wondered at, if he was innately though unin-
tentionally selfish, and utterly regardless of the
feelings of the wife, whose sympathies he never
had ? Mrs. Travers, Sen'r. also did all she could
to foment the dissensions which constantly arose between the two who should have been as *one*. Even
the birth of a daughter failed to cement a breach,
which widened every day. A son would have
been welcomed with joy by the family, as heir to
estates entailed in the male line, but a girl was
considered as a useless and expensive incumbrance,
by all but the young mother herself.

After the birth of my little god-daughter, coldness and indifference became actual dislike. Evelyn and her husband scarcely ever spoke, and a virtual separation took place between them. I remained some time at the Abbey, being loth to leave my friend under such trying circumstances. Evelyn endeavored to beguile the time by cultivating her taste for music; we also studied together various volumes, both of ancient and modern history, and even sounded the depths of natural philosophy and astronomy. Poetry and light literature, she said, made her melancholy, as they portrayed untrue pictures of life—especially with regard to love and marriage. She never would be persuaded to peruse any tale which finished happily; but stories of misfortune, ending in separation or death, she read with avidity.

This was a most unhealthy state of mind. Evelyn's feelings were exceedingly embittered towards her mother and stepfather, whom she considered to have occasioned the terrible mistake of her life. Her husband she pitied with a feeling akin to contempt, knowing that, with a common-place wife, he might have become a better and a happier man, but confessing herself totally unsuited to him. She would not, however, attempt in any way to brighten his path; neither would she endeavor to wean him from his intemperate habits, which, unhappily, became daily more confirmed. I could not but blame, though my heart bled for poor Evelyn; for I felt that, sooner or later, she would learn how that for each and all of our wrong doings, and even for our sins of omission, a just retribution awaits us, either here or hereafter.

CHAPTER VII.

PRESENTATION TO THE QUEEN.

THE drama of real life, like that represented nightly on the mimic stages of our theatres, naturally divides itself into acts and scenes. Will our kind and gracious readers be pleased to imagine themselves now sitting before the drop-curtain, which has just closed over the first act of our piece? In order to put them into an indulgent humor, let fancy place them in the best and most commodious of private boxes, where, ensconced in the most luxurious of lounges, and (if a lady) looking most charming in an opposite mirror, they may placidly and patiently await the rising of the curtain. Then let my fair and friendly reader turn, in imagination, to the play book, and find that a period of some ten years is supposed to have elapsed between the first and second acts of our drama; let her point this out to her companion, whom we will suppose to be *the* gentleman without whom even the most interesting plot would prove insipid. Then let the fair lady and her admirer turn to our little stage, and give us their undivided attention.

The curtain slowly rises, disclosing a gay and brilliant scene, the presence chamber at the Court of Victoria—that lady, even more royal by her virtues, than through her exalted position, though that were of the highest ever filled by woman. Graceful and gracious stands the Queen, to receive the homage of the fairest and the noblest of the land. Her royal husband is beside her, in the prime of manly beauty. In a semi-circle, glittering with diamonds, and gold, and scarlet, stand the illustrious princes and princesses of the blood ; and still farther in the background, appears a scarcely less dazzling group of court beauties and gallant cavaliers in attendance upon the royal party. The beauteous Duchess of Wellington, whose long dark lashes veil eyes whose lustre sorrow and disappointment have somewhat dimmed ; the brilliant Lady Jocelyn, the queenly Duchess of Southerland, all are there in attendance on their beloved Sovereign. The *coup d'œuil* is splendid ; but few who pass before that august circle dare raise their eyes to admire it. A moment, and the Lord Chamberlain receives a card, and announces the name of a lady to be presented to her Majesty. The lady, robed in white, steps gracefully forward, and makes a deep and respectful obeisance to the Queen ; another, equally graceful, but somewhat less humble to the royal circle, and then backing slowly out of the presence chamber, receives the train on her arm from a page in waiting—when, no longer under the immediate eye of majesty, she is permitted to walk in the manner which nature intended. A whisper of admiration is heard from many a young scion of nobility and officer present.

" How beautiful !"

" Who is she ?"

" She must be a married woman."

" Ah ! it is the new Russian Princess they talk so much about."

" No—it is Baroness What's-her-name—you know who I mean—they say the Duke of Devonshire is smitten with her."

" I say, Melville, who *is* that pretty creature ?"

The young guardsman either did not, or would not reply, though he soon set the matter at rest by advancing toward the fair object of all this cross-fire.

" How are you, Mrs. Travers ?" said he. " Allow me to pilot you through the crowd."

" Thank you, Col. Melville—I shall most gladly avail myself of your escort to my carriage."

"How did you get through the presentation?"

"Very well. Her Majesty appeared in a most gracious mood, and the Prince looked splendidly handsome."

"As *you* do to-day—*you* are the true Queen of the drawing-room." Then, in a lower voice—"Oh, Evelyn, let us hasten from this place. I cannot bear that another than myself should even see you, now that our time together is so short."

"We shall meet again ere long I trust," she replied.

"With what coolness and indifference you speak of our parting. Ah, it was not so when at Woodlands you—"

Evelyn's cheek flushed, and her eyes took a displeased expression.

"How selfish you men are! You well know that I am not going abroad for my own pleasure, but that I am ordered to Italy to recruit my health.— Why, then, blame me for that which is inevitable?"

"Blame *you*, Evelyn?" and the young heart throbbed, and the earnest eyes filled with a sorrowful indignation.

The two walked on in silence—and never did mortal pair, since the days of our first parents, appear outwardly more suited to each other.

Evelyn is still all that we have painted her in

early life—though the varying blush of girlhood has given place to the fresh bloom of matured womanhood, and the figure once slight to a fault has acquired that voluptuous roundness, united with grace peculiar to the women of Andalusia—for Evelyn's mother was of Spanish extraction. Col. Melville is the perfect type of an aristocratic Englishman—tall and muscular, yet slight; of a noble military bearing, and a face whose faultless regularity of feature might rival even with that of his fair companion; hair of a light brown, curling naturally like the locks of " the god of the etherial bow ;" whiskers of the same shade; deep-set eyes, where sincerity sat enthroned—and a countenance expressive of goodness and feeling, still flushed with the glow of youth.

Such is the description of the cavalier, leaning on whose manly arm, our heroine threaded her way through the crowded reception rooms of the Palace of St. James.

" Mrs. Travers' carriage stops the way," cries a voice outside.

The name is taken up, and re-echoed again and again, till it is given as " Travers' carriage," " Travers' Brougham," " Towers' coming out."

Evelyn, hastily cloaking, has sprung into her Clarence, but not before a tender glance and a bewitching smile, accompanied by a hurried "you will dine with me to-morrow, my last evening," has quite restored the young guardsman to equanimity.

Let us leave our heroine to the society of her own thoughts, and look once more through memory's glass into the long vista of the past. Many characters who have once figured in these pages, are now no longer living. Mrs. Dale has died, a heart-broken woman, most ungratefully treated by the husband for whom she had sacrificed her child, and her own, and much of her daughter's fortune. The by no means disconsolate widower shortly after married one of the most devoted of his many female worshippers—and his present wife rivals, it is said, even that great saint in sanctity. The good old Squire has gone to his final account. Peace be with his ashes !—for his vices were born of circumstance, his virtues were his own.

Evelyn is now a widow. Let us drop a veil over the closing scenes of the life of one whose deathbed was invaded by the baleful spectres of delirium tremens. Let us hope that, though disliking her husband, the wife shrank not from her duty when the poor sufferer's moans resounded through the chamber of sickness. I have reason to know Evelyn was dissatisfied with herself, when the end came—at last unexpectedly, almost suddenly : but I will fain hope she judged too harshly her involuntary short-comings. I know, also, that if she in any way failed in her duty, her sin has not remained unpunished.

Old Mrs. Travers still lives, or rather vegetates, like some elderly animal of the feline species, who passes her time in spitting at any more juvenile pussy who ventures across her august path. She has gone to live—I know not where, and care still less. Sweet Woodlands, no longer the abode of a Travers, has passed to a very distant connexion of the family. Evelyn consequently is still condemned to be without kith and kin in the world. When, therefore, under the advice of the family physician, she decided on a prolonged sojourn in Italy, a letter was at once despatched to secure myself as a travelling companion. I was then, and am still—shall I confess it?—AN OLD MAID—for I was past thirty, and unmarried.

I gladly accepted Evelyn's proposal to accompany her, but made it a condition that little Ella, her only child, should be my especial charge, thus relieving her mother of some little care and responsibility.

The evening preceding our departure, we dined at our hotel, in company with Colonel Reginald Melville; and, as he had politely brought us a box for Covent Garden, we left instantly after dinner, in order not to lose the commencement of the opera.

Whilst my ears were drinking in the magnificent harmonies of the " *Benediction des Poignards*," in the Huguenots, and my breath was suspended as the delicious tones of the matchless Mario rang through the house, in the exquisite final *duo*, I naturally turned to Evelyn, whom I knew to be passionately fond of music as myself, and to be even a better judge of it scientifically than I am, I met her entranced look : but I saw that Colonel Melville had eyes and ears only for her.

> " She was his sight ;
> For his eye saw with hers, and followed hers ;
> Which colored all his objects—she was his life,
> The ocean to the river of his thoughts,
> Which terminated all."

There was a subdued sorrow in his look, which touched me deeply. Does she love him ? I thought, as I watched her bright and beaming glance, all untroubled by the thought of the morrow's parting ; or, can it be that she is heartless, the friend of my youth, whom I have loved, and still love so dearly ? Methinks, if she *have* a heart, she cannot but be touched by a devotion so deep. Oh, true woman—

"In our hours of ease,
Uncertain, coy, and hard to please,"

Who can fathom the depths of thy soul? My sympathies from that night were with Melville, and I determined any influence I might have over Evelyn, should be exerted in favor of this, her true knight.

CHAPTER VIII.

FOREIGN TRAVEL.

On the very loveliest of summer mornings, in the leafy month of June, Evelyn and myself, with the little fair-haired Ella, a maid, and a courier, started by the mail train for Dover. We were in the highest spirits, and anticipated much enjoyment in our projected journey.

If a shade of tender melancholy lingered on the cheek of my fair companion, at the thought of her recent parting with a handsome and devoted admirer, it was soon dissipated as she called to mind his promise to join us, either at Venice or Florence, as soon as his military duties would permit him to take advantage of the usual autumn regimental leave.

Our journey through "*la belle France*" was a hurried one. Our first halt was at Vevay, on the Lake of Geneva. Here we remained a few days, enjoying the view of the snow-capped mountains—

Mont Blanc, like a hoary giant, faintly discerned in the distance. We made a pilgrimage to "Sweet Clarens," rendered far more interesting through the graphic pen of our own immortal Byron, than as the abode of that disgusting sensualist — Rousseau, whose writings, (such of them, at least, as I have seen), I utterly abhor.

I may be permitted here to remark, that, apart from its exquisite poetic beauties, we found Childe Harolde the best and truest of descriptive guide books, for a work of true genius in poetry as in music, though capable of satisfying the highest intellectual requirements, is also adapted to interest and please the million.

At Vevay we engaged a vetturino to take us over the magnificent Simplon pass to the head of the Lake of Como, whence we intended crossing in the steamer to the town, which takes its name from the lake, and is situated at its lower extremity.

The pass of the Simplon presents to the traveller every variety of scenery, from the verdant and flowery valley, with its murmuring brook and rich pasturage, to the rugged and barren heights, where eternal snow usurps the place of vegetation, and the ear is constantly assailed by the crash of the avalanche, as it leaps from crag to crag and is finally lost in some unfathomable abyss, into whose depths the sun never penetrates.

Our journey usually commenced at sunrise. Having taken a cup of coffee, or a glass of delicious new milk, we entered the carriage, enjoying the exquisite freshness and fragrance of the morning air. At about eleven, a two-hours' rest for the horses brought us to some shady road-side inn, where a breakfast of mountain trout, fresh caught from the stream, and perhaps a chamois cutlet awaited us. Much less tempting fare would, as my readers may imagine, have had ample justice done to it, under such favorable circumstances for exciting an appetite.

Between one and two our second start was made. Our route, perhaps, then led through a forest of pines, rendered doubly aromatic by the magnetism of the sun's beams; or, it might be, the bed of a torrent skirted our path, which we had more than once to cross, on the most picturesque of bridges. The road over this grandly terrible pass is sufficiently wide to admit of two *diligences* passing abreast, without any danger of falling down the awful precipice, which ever yawns on one side of the road, and sometimes on either. To construct such a route over such a mountain, it required the genius of a Napoleon to conceive and to execute;

and each step taken by the Alpine traveller, whe
ther his way lie over the Splugen, the Cenis, or the
still finer and more easy Simplon pass, must raise
his admiration for the herculean labors of this wonder-working architect.

Between five and six, we halted for the night,
probably in the vicinity of some cataract, the rushing of whose waters lulled us to that sweet sleep
which was ever ready to come to our pillow. As
far as my experience goes, these little way-side inns,
frequented by *vetturini* are by far the cleanest,
best, and cheapest I ever entered; and from our
large city hotels, I have frequently looked back to
their homely comforts with regret.

Our prolonged journey permitted my turning the
conversation, occasionally, on Colonel Melville. I
learned from Evelyn, that her acquaintance with
him commenced in rather a romantic manner. He
was hunting in their neighborhood, and in taking a
leap, his horse fell with him, and he had the misfortune to break his leg. Captain Travers, who witnessed the accident, ordered Melville to be carried
to Woodlands, where, unable to be moved without
risk, he remained for six weeks confined to his bed.
Evelyn tended him through his illness, and a strong
sympathy springing up between them, he became a
constant and welcome guest at the Abbey, until old

Mrs. Travers, lynx-eyed as are most dowagers, perceiving a growing attachment between the parties, persuaded her son to be rude to Melville, and to suspect the prudence of his wife. Provoked at her mother-in-law's ill-nature, and angry at the unjust aspersions of her husband, Evelyn confessed that she had kept up a clandestine correspondence with the young man, by letter, and also had occasionally met him alone in the park. She added, that, aware of her unhappiness, Melville had presumed even to speak to her of marriage, should she ever regain her freedom. Since her widowhood, however, she told me she had forbidden him ever to allude to the subject of their future union till a decent time should have elapsed since the death of her husband.

I was glad to receive her confidence, but thought it my duty to chide her imprudence, in permitting herself, as a married woman, clandestine meetings with an avowed lover. I showed her, that however innocent her feelings and intentions, her husband would have had a right to suspect the worst, adding that even to Col. Melville she had given but too much occasion to think lightly of her discretion, but that I trusted having proved that she loved him to the very verge of imprudence, she would later become to him the most faithful and modest of wives.

Whatever reply Evelyn might have made, was cut short by Ella's exclamation—

"See, mama! how lovely!"

We looked—and there lay the beauteous Como, with her waters of sapphire, sparkling as if gemmed with a thousand diamonds, in the beams of the mid-day sun, her banks studded with innumerable villas, white as Parian marble. We reached Colico in time to take the steamer to the foot of the lake. At the small town of Como we found the train waiting to convey us to Milan.

I will not here detain my readers to describe the fine Cathedral, with its lofty dome, filled with that "dim religious light," which insensibly recalls us from the multiform distractions of daily life, and disposes the mind to devotion. I pity the man who could enter such an edifice without breathing a prayer, however short, to the Author of all good. I do not envy him, if he could leave that sacred building, and not feel, at least momentarily, the desire to become " a wiser and a better man."

We remained but one day in Milan—just glanced at Padua, Mantua, Verona—all interesting cities in themselves, but still more so from the association of their names in the divine comedies of the "sweet swan of Avon," our own immortal Shakespeare.— These fair cities were powerless to arrest our steps.

4

A fever was upon our spirits, which brooked not delay—and wherefore? Beautiful city of my dreams! thou "sea Cybele," rising from the blue waters of the Adriatic, with thy numerous palaces and thy countless spires, gleaming so white in the pure Italian moonlight—was it not to look upon thy loveliness as in a vision, that we pressed onward, and still onward, as the young lover to greet his beloved. The stormy ocean kisses thy marble feet in homage—wert thou not his bride of old?— Thou most silent Queen, dost thou mourn in voiceless grief the decay of thy sculptured halls, once so brilliant in the festive scene, ere yet untrodden by the armed heel of the ruthless Saxon? Or dost thou weep in thy desolation for thy dark-eyed sons, whose godlike brows are bowed down, and whose cheeks pale beneath the yoke of the stranger? Oh, Garibaldi! hero of the lion heart, how long wilt thou leave her in her anguish, a slave amid slaves!

Fairy-like and unreal appeared that city to us, and yet so like my young imaginings, that I sometimes doubted whether I actually beheld fair Venice with my waking eyes. Those hearse-like gondolas, how silently do they thread the streets; only the ceaseless plash of the water is heard on the steps of the palaces—now, alas! crumbling into ruins. Look-

ing on the Piazza di San Marco, I could not divest
myself of the idea that I beheld a scene at the opera—there was the Basilico, the costumes, the moonlight—all that I had seen so frequently portrayed at
Covent Garden, and her Majesty's theatre. Nor
was music wanting to complete the illusion. Airs
from Marino Faliero, Othello, and other familiar
strains, were played by the Austrian band; and as
we sipped our coffee, or ate our ices, seated under
the trees in this beautiful piazza, Evelyn would declare that it was not possible to live at Venice without an *Amoroso*, and even my old maidhood
confessed that the softly voluptuous breezes, the
dream-like beauty of the city, the seclusion of the
gondolas—all spake to the fancy, of love, mystery,
and romance.

CHAPTER IX.

FLORENCE.

SUMMER had now given place to Autumn, with its treasures of corn and wine; not that pallid season, half-summer, half-winter, of our more northern climes—but the glowing Autumn of Italy, when the purple clusters of grapes hang pendent from the trellised arbor of vine-leaves over-head; when the orange groves are fragrant with their golden fruit, and the luscious fig and dark olive grove invite the traveller to refreshment and repose.

On quitting Venice, we had decided on retracing our steps, in order to visit the cities we had not yet seen. From Genoa we followed the beautiful coast road to Pisa, whence we took rail to Florence, arriving there towards the latter part of September. We thus had time to visit the various galleries and artistic curiosities of the city of the Medici, previously to the commencement of the fashionable season, when Florence is usually thronged with

strangers. We engaged a fine apartment—"primo
piano"—(first floor) on the Lungo L'Arno, considered the best situation by strangers, though not by
the Florentines themselves, who call it unhealthy.
Nor are they wrong—for the Arno, like the Tiber,
is a yellow, dirty stream, unpoetic to the eye, and
frequently most unsavory to another sense. Florence
nevertheless well deserves her name of "La bella."
The town is built on either side of the river, which
is spanned by five exquisitely light and well pro-
portioned bridges, each of which differs in the style
of its architecture from the others. These bridges
unite the two cities as it were into one. As is usual,
one side of the river monopolizes the rank and fashion of Florence, although the grand ducal palace of
Pitti is situate on its opposite and quieter border.
Our first visit was of course to the "Palazzo d'egli
Uffigiis," to view the celebrated Venus de Medicis. We expected much, and were therefore of
course disappointed. The figure is artistically
perfect ; perhaps this very perfection causes the
effect to be cold and unsympathetic. The face, too,
is entirely without expression. She resembles rather a young nymph of Diana than the goddess of
love and beauty, whose voluptuous charms are far
better portrayed in the statue called the Venus of

the Capitol in Rome—infinitely superior, in my opinion, to her Florentine sister.

At the Pitti Palace, we spent hours wrapped in silent contemplation before that superhuman painting, the divine Madonna della Seggiola of Raphael Sanzio. Most of my readers will be familiar with the copies of this picture, but these, one and all will give them but a very imperfect idea of the original, *which cannot be reproduced*. The features and complexion may, it is true, be copied—but who but the immortal Raphael could represent the infinitely tender and happy, yet half wondering look of the young mother, as she clasps that mysterious Babe to her virgin breast! Who but he might portray those dove-like eyes, welling over with maternal love? Verily it was given to that wondrous poet-painter alone to reveal to mortal sight the spotless Mary, who "kept all these things, and pondered them in her heart." And even he must have used as his brush a plume fresh plucked from an angel's wing, all bright and glowing with the hues of Paradise. Observe, too, the look of thought, far beyond his years, which almost casts the shadow of coming sorrow over the baby brow of that divine Infant. Genius, highest gift of heaven! how glorious are thy works!—how godlike thy mission upon earth!

Strangers were now fast pouring into Florence, and the winter was expected to be unusually brilliant. Col. Melville arrived, and became the constant companion of our walks and drives, and a welcome guest at our dinner table. Evelyn treated him kindly—at times almost as an accepted lover, whilst at others she appeared to weary of his society, and to long for change and excitement. Highly fitted to shine in the *salon*, and passionately fond of amusement, our heroine had never, as yet, been able fully to gratify her taste for the world, which from the very novelty of its pleasures to her, now became her idol. An all-engrossing affection, it may be imagined, like that of Melville, rather nettled and annoyed her; she hated restraint, desired to be uncontrolled mistress of her actions, to dance when and with whom she pleased, and to accept the homage of the favored few. I will do her the justice to say she never cared to attract the notice of the million, and had a perfect horror of the street admiration so usual on the Continent.

Melville was jealous. He could not view with calmness the smiles of the lady of his love lavished on another. He would leave the room—perhaps the house—and not return, till a small, rose-colored missive would once again recall him to the side of his fair tormentor.

With all this, Evelyn was not a deliberate coquette. She admired and esteemed Melville, and
appreciated his devotion with her whole heart—but
unhappily she fell into that fatal mistake common to
beauties, that affection such as his, is of every
day occurrence, and to be considered merely as the
meed due to her charms. How frequently do the
lovely of our sex thus make shipwreck of their happiness, not knowing how *very few* are capable of
feeling the true sentiment of love, and how priceless
therefore is the heart of an honorable man. Alas!
in bitter suffering, and with tears of blood, do they
expiate their supreme folly!—they then, when too
late, perceive how they have flung away the purest
gold for mere tinsel, and now they must starve for
the want of that bread of life which can alone satisfy the famished heart, and which that once despised gold would have purchased.

The plain woman is wiser. *She* does not trample
on the heart that loves her; and thus her lot is frequently a brighter one than that of her fairer,
though less fortunate sister, doomed to mourn in
silence and loneliness the neglected happiness of
the past.

What would that weary one now give for one
glance, in which soul answers to soul—for one word
uttered even in reproach, by lips which, in the past,

breathed but tenderness and love? Alas, alas!—it is too late—*too late*—and the haughty and once-petted beauty is forever alone with the spectre of by-gone days!

Like all women who have been accustomed to much attention from the opposite sex, Evelyn looked for impossibilities. The future husband her fancy painted, was to unite high station and wealth, and every advantage of mind and person, with, of course, a heart entirely devoted to her. "That love," says the Hon. Mrs. Norton, in her beautiful and romantic novel, "Stuart of Dunleith," "which at once satisfies the soul, the intellect, the heart and the senses, is met with once, and once only in life." I quote from memory, and consequently express the sentiments of the gifted author in my own words. But, is it so? *I think not.* Perfect happiness is not to be found on earth; therefore, let my lady readers be content, if they meet one who unites three—aye, even two of these requisites, combined with sincere attachment— let her not then despise her lover, but rather wear him in her heart of hearts.

The grand ducal court of Florence was, at the time we were there, one of the pleasantest and most aristocratic *réunions* of aristocratic Europe. Any stranger, once presented there by his minister, was

4*

invited to all the balls, concerts, and receptions which were given weekly through the entire winter season.

The Grand Duke Leopold, a most excellent old man, and greatly beloved by a large circle of the nobility, was adored by the poor, whose sick-beds he frequently visited in person. The Grand Duchess, his consort, a Princess of Naples, though much younger than her husband, had ever borne a perfectly unblemished reputation. Her imperial highness was a remarkably fine woman, with the most beautifully-formed shoulders I ever beheld. She was most gracious, and at the same time dignified in her manners, and always had a kind and affable word for the ladies whom she recognized as frequent attendants at her receptions.

The youthful imperial family were worthy of their royal parents. The two elder Arch-Dukes, although mere boys, were distinguished in the ball-room for their graceful and amiable manners, and for their skill in the dance, of which they were passionately fond, as is usual with youths of their age. The heir-apparent had lately brought home his young and beautiful bride, a Princess of Saxony. Alas! who could have imagined, in a few short years, that lovely girl would be laid in an early grave!—this august family would be forever exiled from their native soil! Even now, I see the poor old man; his white hairs, powerless to protect him from insult, bowed down with sorrow—yet struggling manfully with his grief, in order to console his weeping consort, Grand Duchess—now in name only. I see the faithful *guardia nobile* press around the carriages, to spare the beloved and venerated family the gibes and sneers of the ladies (women are ever the most cruel) who had so frequently partaken of their sovereign's hospitality, but who now were congregated at the gate of the city, to smile at a misfortune which, however possible its ultimate benefits to Italy, had fallen on innocent heads.

The government of Leopold of Tuscany was almost of too paternal a character. There were literally no police. I never heard of any spies; and the obnoxious Austrian soldiers had long been sent back to their own country. *Why* the Florentines preferred their country being turned into a province of Piedmont, and governed by a Viceroy, instead of remaining an independent State, I am at a loss to imagine; nor can I make out wherefore they disliked their excellent Sovereign and his amiable family. No good has, for the present, resulted from their bloodless revolution. Let us, however, hope the day may dawn, which will see fair Italy once more a nation, united under one head. Then, perhaps, Florence herself may derive the benefit she has not yet reaped from her change of rulers.

CHAPTER X.

COQUETRY.

ALL Florence was talking of the *Bal Costumé* to be given at the *Casino de' Nobili* to H. R. H. the Count of Syracuse, a Neapolitan Prince, brother to the Grand Duchess, and at present on a visit to his Imperial sister at the Palazzo Pitti. The ladies were endeavoring each to outvie the other in the novelty and richness of their costumes. The Grand Ducal family were to represent their ancient predecessors on the throne of Florence, the rich and princely family of Medici. The notorious and once lovely Lady C—— F——, it was known would appear as Pomona, her dress to be looped up with bunches of fruit interspersed with diamonds, to represent the dew. A beautiful Florentine duchess, it was whispered, would personify the " Queen of Hearts;" but so well did her modiste keep the secret that none could guess either the fashion or color of her robe, which proves that women *can* be trusted, at least in so im-

portant an affair as that of the toilette. Counting
on her fresh beauty, and conscious that she could
not hope to out-blaze her fair rivals in jewelry,
Evelyn wisely preferred to be unique in the simplicity of her costume. She therefore chose the becoming dress of a peasant girl of Frascati, in the
environs of Rome. Her corset of cherry-colored
velvet, laced over a chemisette of plaited muslin,
displayed to advantage the rounded waist and perfectly modelled shoulders. The full petticoat of blue
silk trimmed with rows of ribbon to match the cor-
sage, just cleared the well-turned ancle, and fully
discovered the little Spanish foot with its arched
instep. The hair, wrapped around the head, was
fastened in a rich knot by two pins of diamond, and
one large brilliant clasped the narrow band of red
velvet which encircled her throat. The peasant's
apron, and bows of ribbon of blue and silver completed a costume in which the wearer looked scarcely more than eighteen. I accompanied my friend
en *Marquise*, as this required but little exercise
of the fancy, in which (as regards dress) I am lament-
ably deficient. Colonel Melville (whose leave ex-
pired very shortly), was to wear the uniform of his
corps, and to meet us at the ball.

Evelyn's toilette was a decided success; a murmur of admiration accompanied us as we threaded

our way through the brilliant crowd of officers and
gaily attired young nobles who thronged the vesti-
bule and ante-rooms of the building. After some
difficulty we succeeded in reaching the upper end
of the ball room, where on a slightly elevated dais
were seated the Imperial family. The Grand Duchess, as the celebrated Catharine de Medicis in a
magnificent costume of the middle ages, was literally one blaze of jewels. On perceiving Evelyn—
who was rather a favorite—she beckoned her to approach, and graciously complimented her on the
good taste and simplicity of her attire. The Count
Syracuse, who was a great admirer of beauty, then
stepped forward and engaged the pretty Frascatana
for a quadrille. The Prince, who, though somewhat
stout, was a remarkably fine looking man, appeared
to the utmost advantage as Lorenzo de Medicis.—
His extremely fascinating manners, together with
his exalted rank, rendered him (if report speak
true) almost irresistible with the female sex. But
he was by no means a constant lover; he might
with truth say, with a celebrated French roué:
" *Moi je suis fidèle à tout le monde.*"

The count devoted himself to his "Cynthia of the
minute," and scarcely left her side, much to the disgust and envy of many a noble signora, who longed
in vain for even one glance of passing admiration

from the illustrious Don Giovanni, who had no eyes
but for his simple Zerlina. Evelyn gave herself up
to the intoxication of gratified vanity, and appeared
to be as much charmed with her royal cavalier as
he was taken with her. Had not the prince been a
married man, I believe she would have aspired even
to an alliance with royalty, for the recent choice
of the French Emperor had contributed to turn the
head of many a beauty. As it was, to permit such
marked attention from a Prince, whose success with ladies was proverbial, could not but be
detrimental to a virtuous woman's reputation. Thus
reflecting, I turned to seek Melville. Poor fellow!
he was leaning against a fluted column the very
statue of despair. In his expressive countenance
you might see depicted all the tortures of jealousy
and mortified pride. I advanced towards him and
touched his elbow. He started as from a dream,
made a few polite and common-place observations,
and before I could speak a word, had vanished from
the room. I still thought he would return, as was
his wont, to escort us to the refreshment table, for
Evelyn's Italian adorers were usually too intently
occupied in discussing the excellent supper and
wines provided by their royal host, to have time to
attend to the wants of any fair lady.

The Count Syracuse was forced to accompany

the Imperial party to supper. He therefore brought his lovely partner all glowing with the triumphs and excitement of the dance to my side. Evelyn passed her arm within mine.

"Let us seek Reginald Melville," said she, "you will doubtless be glad of some refreshment."

"Ah! dear Evelyn," I replied, "I fear your imprudent coquetry has caused much suffering tonight."

"He is foolish to be so jealous," replied she; "does he wish me to speak to no one, and to make myself disagreeable in society?"

"But to remain so long with one man," I remonstrated.

"Oh! a *Prince*, you know; how could I refuse? Indeed, Melville is most unreasonably exacting, and you encourage him. I should detest so jealous a husband. No; if he cannot bear to see a woman admired, let him choose a plain wife."

Her levity vexed me, for I could not imagine a pleasure that necessarily entailed pain upon others. But then, remember, *I am not a beauty*.

We sought Melville in every room; he was nowhere to be found. Evelyn was evidently piqued; she became *distraite*, and answered at random the various compliments and observations addressed to her. She refused all invitations to dance, and had

Melville now seen her, the destiny of two lives might
have been changed. How often do we of the weaker sex wrap ourselves in our woman's pride and
carefully conceal our true feelings from the being
we respect and esteem most upon earth. How frequently even in our moments of apparent cruelty
and caprice do we in the depth of our soul resolve
one day by the devotion of a life to make full and
ample amends for the momentary pangs we may
have caused! Thrice happy they who may be permitted to put these good resolves into practice ere
it be *too late.*

We remained but a short time at the now distasteful ball. On the morrow Evelyn had a nervous
headache and kept her room. Although she had
given orders that no one was to be admitted, I perceived her look of disappointment when the name
of Colonel Melville was missing from the pile of
cards and notes brought by her maid in the evening
to her bedside.

The following day, being quite restored, she
arose and dressed with more than usual care
and good taste. I saw that she expected Melville
would call, that being his last day in Florence, and
I doubted not that when he came all would go well
—and I might have to congratulate two happy
affianced lovers. Evelyn was restless and abstract-

ed. She tried to sing, but was out of voice; she took up a book, but did not get farther than the title-page; her eyes wandered perpetually towards the French *pendule* on the mantel-piece ; at last she rose impatiently, and stated her intention of driving to the Cascines, that loveliest of promenades, unsurpassed even by the far-famed " Bois de Boulogne."

At that moment there was a loud ring at the entrance door of the apartment. My heart beat in sympathy with that of Evelyn, who turned pale as death. The servant did not at once answer the door—five long minutes of suspense, and the ring was again repeated. At length the door was opened. A manly step was heard, and H. R. H. the Count of Syracuse entered.

Evelyn trembled visibly, but mastered her emotion, and received her royal visitor with graceful dignity. Though I perceived the Prince greatly desired my absence, I thought it wiser to remain with my friend, whose agitation I feared might be interpreted too favorably.

About ten minutes after the Prince's arrival, another ring at the bell was heard. This time a well-known voice enquired—

" Is Mrs. Travers at home ?"

A short colloquy with the servant followed, and

we heard the door of the apartment closed. I looked towards Evelyn. Her vexation was so evident
that the Prince asked if she were ill. I was obliged
to come to the rescue—and declared, with truth,
that she had kept her room the preceding day, and
was scarcely sufficiently recovered to do the honors
to His Royal Highness.

The Count took the hint, and paid us that time
but a short visit. The moment he had quitted, the
servant brought in on a small waiter, Col. Melville's card, with P. P. C. in the corner. We ques-
tioned the man—

"Did the Colonel say he would call again ?"

"No, signora."

"Did he state when he was leaving ?"

"No, signora."

"Well then, what *did* he say ?" I exclaimed,
wishing to spare Evelyn the pain of asking.

"The Colonel asked if the signora was alone. I
told him Sna. Altezza Reale was with the signora.
The signore then said, Give this card to the signora.
That is all, ladies."

It was then near five, the hour of departure
of the train. The servant was sent to inquire if
the Colonel left that evening. He returned with
the message—"*Il Colonello è partito già*"—"the Colonel is already gone."

Evelyn's disappointment turned to anger. Her pride was offended, and she determined to punish Melville by encouraging the visits of her Royal admirer—a very dangerous game!

> " For slander's mark was ever yet the fair,
>   The ornament of beauty is suspect,
>   A crow that flies in heaven's sweetest air."

Her charms and success had made our heroine many enemies, especially among her own sex, and envious tongues were busy with her fair fame. She was termed a heartless jilt, and her conduct towards Melville was commented on in the severest terms.

In Italy no woman ought to permit any marked attention from one of the opposite sex, if she would preserve an unblemished reputation. The innocent frankness of my countrywomen, and of the American ladies, is liable to be sadly misconstrued by the idle and languid Italian " lions," who lounge away their time at the doors of the different cafes, and discuss the appearance and character of the ladies, as they pass in their carriages toward the Lungo L'Arno and Cascines.

Evelyn, whose conduct had been, and still was, most indiscreet, being, moreover, without a protector, was especially the mark for scandal. Women who would have given the world to have

been able to do as she did, were the first to blame
her imprudence ; and the young Florentine exquisites, who had never yet succeeded in winning a smile
from " *la bella Inglese*," now invented all kinds of
cruel and false reports concerning her.   The frequent visits of the Count Syracuse were reported
to the Grand Duchess, who henceforth looked cold-
ly upon Evelyn, and the ladies of society were only
too happy to have it in their power to mortify one
who had excited their jealousy.   And Melville, too
—the good, the kind, the loving—had he also deserted the woman he once held so dear ? The next
chapter may perhaps throw some light on this subject.

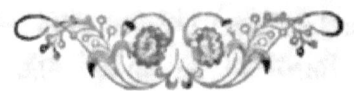

CHAPTER XI.

FIRST LOVE.

COLONEL REGINALD MELVILLE TO EVELYN TRAVERS.

London, February 28th.

BEFORE you receive this, Evelyn, I shall be far away; it may, perhaps, cost you one pang in the midst of your triumphs, to know that we are at last parted; it may be for years—it may be *forever*.

My regiment is under immediate orders for India, and we sail in a week. We are required to quell the Sepoy rebellion, and to avenge the horrible brutalities perpetrated by those savages on our innocent countrywomen and their helpless babes. I will not, at this supreme moment, reproach you—your naturally good heart will teach you how far you have erred—but I will simply mention how deeply I felt your inconsiderate conduct at the last ball, when you knew that, in two days, one who loved you as his own soul must leave; and how still more bitterly was I disappointed at having been

prevented by the prince's presence from bidding you
a last adieu.

You are very beautiful and talented. It is natural you should command attention wherever you
go. But, oh! Evelyn, does this satisfy your heart?
Ask yourself, are you not sometimes unhappy, even
amid the most brilliant scenes? Do not imagine
that every fop who approaches you, is capable of
sincere attachment, even to a creature as fascinating as yourself. You are, to the majority of
men, but as the pastime of an idle hour—or worse,
the coquette whose smiles flatter their selfish vanity,
and of whose favors they boast at the public promenades or the *cafés*. But of this I cannot bear to
speak—even the thought is madness.

It is true, alas! that I dare not hope that one so
gifted and so adored, will await the uncertainties
of war, and mourn, in some retired corner of the
earth, the absence of a future husband. No, Evelyn—I deeply feel the vanity of entertaining such a
hope, even for a moment. I know, too well, you
will meet those who will hang on each word, and
watch every look, as I have done. You will *never*
forget me; but I shall share your heart with others.
It is for this, therefore, that I am resolved, cost what
it will, and at the risk of breaking my heart,
to utter this fatal word—Farewell, then, beloved of

my soul—my first, my only love—*you are free.*
Think of me, henceforth, as a tender brother. I
will ever cherish you as a sister. For your own
sake, and that of your dear Ella, be prudent;
remember that a woman's name should never even
be breathed upon.

One more effort—one more bitter pang, and my
self-imposed duty is done. If ever my sweet sister
should find one who loves her as I do—but who,
unlike poor Melville, approaches near to the standard of perfection she has erected in her own imagination—then, dearest, do not hesitate to become his
wife. My prayers shall ever be offered up for your
happiness; and you, my ever-beloved Evelyn, will
not, even in the midst of that bliss, refuse—if I
fall—to drop a tear for one who would die to save
you even one moment's uneasiness. Farewell—
farewell! R. M.

EVELYN TRAVERS TO REGINALD MELVILLE.

Castellamare, Villa des Alberi, 5th May.

I have been seriously ill, dear Reginald, or you
would have heard from me ere this. I left Florence
a week after I received your letter; and the
fatigues of the journey, added to the violent shock
consequent on the receipt of such sad news, quite

overcame me. I was taken with a nervous trembling, which ended in fever. For two months
I have been confined to my room, and strictly forbidden to write, read, or even to think. I have,
however, succeeded in persuading my doctor, that
to remain alone with my regrets for the past is
retarding indefinitely my recovery. He has, therefore, permitted me to write these few lines to
you.

And are we, then, really to be parted *forever?*
Oh! my once kind Reginald, why condemn me to
live without your love! I see at last the folly and
madness of sacrificing a true attachment for the
heartless and aimless admiration of the passing
hour. Oh! how lonely do I feel now in the world—
how its hollowness wearies me! Sweet Ella even
seems to reproach my frivolity with her calm angel
eyes; nor can I endure Mary's face of grave and sad
reproof.

Reginald, if you ever loved me, write and say
that I am forgiven—tell me that I have not ruined
your happiness. Do not speak of my poor attractions. Would that I were plain, since my beauty
has caused our separation.

You say you are not my "*beau ideal.*" If it be
true, that my foolish romantic fancy has portrayed
an impossible hero—at least, your rare devotion to

one worthless as myself is the very "*beau ideal*" of all that mortals term love. For this, accept my undying gratitude.

One last request—for your Evelyn's sake, be prudent. Do not expose yourself to danger unnecessarily; and she will nightly kneel before the throne of grace, and pray that her numerous faults and follies may rather be visited on her own head, and that every blessing, temporal and eternal, may fall to the lot of him who, though absent, is forever present with his repentant

EVELYN.

P. S.—Remember, I shall count the days, the hours, the moments, until I hear from you. Do not keep me in suspense. Mary desires kindest regards, and little Ella her best love.

After the preceding letter was dispatched to Colonel Melville's agents for transmission to India, I endeavored as much as possible to divert Evelyn's mind from dwelling on painful subjects. The state of her health was far from satisfactory. I therefore used all my influence to persuade her to enter a little into society, as we calculated no reply could possibly come under three months from the seat of war, and till that time had elapsed anxiety would be but needless self-torment. We

were acquainted with an English family, whose
pretty schooner—the "Turquoise"—was lying in
the bay of Sorento. Captain and Mrs. Blake had
frequently invited us to make excursions with them
to the various objects of interest which abound on
the classic shores of the ancient Parthenope. We
had hitherto refused—myself because I detested the
sea; Evelyn, because she was utterly out of spirits.
One evening, however, our kind friends came and
would take no denial. They were accompanied by
a young Sicilian nobleman, a great friend of Ella's,
for he never called without a box of bonbons, a bas-
ket of fruit, or a bouquet for the young lady, whom
he had named *Sorcietto*, or "little Mousey." The
Duc di Balzano was a fine-looking man of from
twenty-eight to thirty years of age. Dark as the very
darkest of his race, he possessed an open countenance, and an expression beaming with goodness.
Unlike the generality of his rather effeminate countrymen, Balzano was cast in the mould of a Her-
cules, and even in England, (that land of splendidly
formed men), he would have been remarked for the
perfection of his figure and the grace of his move-
ments. I remember later seeing him execute the
Tarentella, or national dance of Naples, in a manner that might have shamed many a Terpsichorean
star of the opera.

Yielding to Ella's entreaties, Evelyn consented to make one of the party, and arranged on the following morning to drive to Sorento and there embark in our friend's yacht. I was excused, as all were aware that a marine excursion was anything but a pleasure to me. It was proposed first to visit the purple cave of Capri, which can only be entered in calm weather and at low tide. Even then the visitor must almost recline in the boat, so low is the entrance to the cave. When this difficulty is passed you are amply repaid by the sight of a lofty dome of rock, spanning a body of water actually of the color of indigo. Great care is necessary in making the visit that no storm is in prospect, for when the waves are high, the imprudent traveler has been unable to return, sometimes for days, in consequence of the exit to the cave having been entirely submerged by the raging element which surrounds it.

Our party entered under favorable auspices, for the sea was calm, though there was at the same time a ground swell, which had made poor Ella very sea-sick, and obliged her to be left on a sofa in the yacht. Ella's indisposition gave rise to a rather amusing adventure which I shall now relate :

On her return on board, Evelyn found the child very ill, so much so as to alarm her mother who went to Captain Blake and begged him to put them instantly ashore.

"My dear lady," replied he, "it is all very well for you to talk, but I know no landing place within some hours' sail."

"Then," besought Evelyn, "let us put back to Sorento."

"Impossible," exclaimed the captain, "the little wind there is, is contrary. It would take us twelve hours to get there."

Just then di Balzano made his appearance, and the poor mother, in despair, began in Italian to explain the circumstances to him. The duke in the kindest manner reassured Captain Blake as to the nature of the coast, and informed Evelyn that although he knew of no *good* landing place near, he would gladly escort her and little Ella in safety home to Castellamare. "But," he added, looking at Evelyn, "the signorina must have a little patience, for we cannot make even the nearest landing place till nightfall."

Gratefully thanking him, Evelyn returned to her daughter, who soon became pacified under the hope of once more being on terra firma.

At eight o'clock, true to his promise, the Captain stopped the schooner, a boat was lowered, and the party entered. Balzano held the sick child in his

arms like a tender nurse. The landing was indeed
far rougher than even he had expected—it was a
regular mountain scramble in the dark. Arrived
at the summit, Ella and her mother were glad to
repose on the floor of the miserable hut appropriat-
ed to the coast guard. On inquiry, they learned
they were eight miles from Sorento, the road thither lying over a mountain ridge, which must be
passed on donkeys. None of these animals, they
were told, were to be had under a two hours' ride
from thence. Balzano at once started in search of
asses, pressing a boy into the service. For nearly
three hours did the poor tired travellers wait in the
smoky atmosphere of the guard-house, the return
of their kind escort. At last the welcome patter of
donkeys' feet was heard, and three sorry beasts
made their appearance. No time was lost in mount-
ing. Balzano, who was dressed in summer costume,
wrapped his plaid around Evelyn, who had placed
her own shawl about the little girl.

The cold on the mountains was excessive, the
path difficult, and there was no moon. At about
two A. M. the party arrived at Sorento; but though
they knocked loudly at the doors of the principal
hotels, no one would rise to admit them. A testy
Englishman only, in a red night-cap, looked out
from a third floor window, and abused them in very

bad Italian for disturbing his slumbers. Evelyn getting angry herself, replied in the same language, which her excitement rendered less melo diously correct than usual. The colloquy greatly amused her cavalier, who laughed heartily at the expense of the *dui Inglese* disputing in bad Italian.

To make a long story short, our friends dismounted, and passed the night in an empty carriage, for the poor donkeys could not, or would not go a step further—and soon after sunrise they persuaded its owner to put horses to the vehicle, thus arriving at our Villa, to my infinite surprise, at about six in the morning.

The suite of this otherwise laughable adventure had well nigh proved fatal to poor Balzano. His kindness and politeness in giving up his plaid when so thinly clothed, caused a severe chill, which ended in a most dangerous attack of fever, in which he nearly lost his life. A strong constitution, and a calm, well-regulated mind, to our infinite relief, enabled our excellent friend eventually and perfectly to recover his health.

CHAPTER XII.

DEATH.

WE had calculated to a nicety the possible time in which we could receive a letter from Reginald Melville, taking into consideration the accidents of wind and water at sea, and the delays and uncertainties on land; but, at length, the time had arrived when each day was a continued torture. Ah! which of us do not remember, at some time of our lives, the dreadful alternations of sickly hope and bitter disappointment we have experienced in waiting for *that letter* so long delayed? Each morning, as we arose, we have said to ourselves— "To-day it will surely come." How we watch the clock! We are quite relieved to hear it is ten minutes too fast: the ten minutes pass—another five also, and we send down to know if the postman is late to-day. We are somewhat consoled to hear that he is occasionally even later. How our heart beats as we see him turn the corner: how dreadfully slow he walks. He stops to speak to some one. Oh! will he *never* cease talking? We feel tempted to fly down and relieve our insupportable anxiety; but a horrible fear we will not confess to ourselves freezes us into stone. No, better wait—it can be but a few moments. The postman goes to the house near by. Happy inmates! One, two— yes, three letters for them. At length he approaches—will he pass by? No, he stops. Two letters. We feel that we shall faint, if they are not brought up at once; yet we dare not go to meet them. Five minutes, which seem an eternity, and the servant enters with the letters. How sick we turn—IT is not there! And this torment we must undergo daily, till a kind Providence guides that long-desired letter to our hands—too often, when it comes, the bearer of ill-tidings, of change, of sickness, of death. Poor mortals! Cruel, indeed, were our destiny, did not the glimpse of a happier morrow brighten for us the deep shadows which envelope the tomb!

Ella, though a mere child in years, shared the anxiety of her mother with almost womanly tenderness. My little god-daughter was a most interesting girl. She was now about eleven years of age, and bore the promise of remarkable loveliness. Like her mother in regularity of feature, she was still of quite a different style of beauty. Her complexion was of that transparent fairness which an artist in order to copy would tinge with a blue shade. Her hair, of the color called in France *blond cendré*, fell in rich wavy masses to her waist. To a casual observer Ella might appear calm—almost cold; but *we* knew her to possess intense feeling beyond her years.

The child had been suffering from slight fever, and was but just convalescent. We had removed to Naples, to procure better medical advice. It was now the month of November; yet the air was balmy as in the first days of Spring. Ella reclined on a couch near the window; her mother, seated near, passed her hand fondly over the splendid hair which quite inundated the pillow and swept the ground. In a few moments the young girl was in a deep sleep. Evelyn still continued to caress her. Turning to me, after a pause, she said : "If I could only know whether Reginald is alive or dead, I think I should be less wretched."

As her mother spoke, I beheld Ella raise herself to a sitting posture. Her eyes were dilated, as if she saw something in the distance. Evelyn, alarmed, would have awaked her; but I motioned her to silence.

The child slowly raised her arm, and pointed with her delicate finger to something she appeared to see; then, in a clear, ringing voice, like and yet unlike her own: "I see a large army move across a plain, like an ocean of verdure. Oh! it is so wide—so wide—the groves of trees are like islands, here and there; and oh, mama, how beautiful! See the palaces, the domes—all gold and azure. See the white columns and terraces. What a lovely place!" She paused a moment; and then, suddenly, almost screamed, catching her mother's arm: "Oh! look—look at that brave officer, on a grey horse—see his white plumes dance. He draws his sword; he fears nothing. Oh! it is—it is Reginald. Reginald, do not go there—there is blood—blood! Mama, take me away! They fight—they are wicked. I will not see this horrible blood!"

Ella covered her eyes, and fell back on the sofa. Her limbs were convulsed, her chest heaved for a few moments, and then happily she sank into a deep and peaceful sleep, in which she remained for some hours. When she awoke, she appeared more cheerful than usual, and seemed to have utterly forgotten her dream—if dream it could be called.

The occurrence was so remarkable, that I wrote it down in my journal, with the date; and later, when I had become familiar with the phenomena of clairvoyance, and the mesmeric trance, I considered this as one of the most remarkable instances of the kind on record.

Another month, and we had almost ceased to hope for the letter. When it came, it was thus:

Before Lucknow, November ——, '57.

Your letter, my beloved Evelyn, I have only just received: through some mistake, it has been lying at my agent's, in Calcutta; and I have only now been able to press it to my heart and lips. Thanks, a thousand thanks, for the sweet hope that letter contains. If God spare this poor life, it shall be devoted to render my Evelyn forever happy. Do not speak of forgiveness; it is I that ought to ask pardon, for having mistrusted the woman I respect and revere most upon earth. Can she forget a foolish jealousy, occasioned by her beauty and fascination? I am making a writing-table out of the stump of a tree. To-morrow, we expect to storm Lucknow. Our chief, Sir Colin, has kindly placed me on his staff.

The thought of you, sweetest, will stimulate me to dare everything. I fervently trust in God that my life may be spared, now that it is of value to you; but if, in the divine decrees of an all-wise Providence, I am fated to fall—then, Evelyn, my wife, before Heaven—farewell! Do not mourn for one who will have died the death of a hero. Shed a few gentle, pitying tears, and then *be happy*, and forget me. No—do not forget. Remember me as one to whom you were dearer than all but his honor—one who will ever watch and guard you, even from that world beyond the tomb, to which we are all hastening. One curl of your soft brown hair and your miniature have never left my heart. If these are returned, you will know that a spirit has passed away, whose last thought in dying was of you. Again, and again—Farewell? God forever bless you, my own—my bride!

Your loving
Reginald.

Short happiness did this letter bring to our hearts. *It* also had been long delayed on the road. Three days after its receipt Evelyn entered my room ere it was day, pale—her hair dishevelled, her eyes red and swelled with weeping.

" Reginald is dead," said she, " I have seen him. Nay, speak not," she added, seeing I would have chided her folly, " I have murdered him. Had I consented to a marriage he would have left the army, and would never have been sent to India. As I lay awake last night, I tell you I saw him as plain as I do you. He approached the bed, looked lovingly upon me, and I saw a wound in his breast. Suddenly the form melted into air. I had no fear. I wished he would again appear. I should have spoken to him. But nothing more occurred."

Evelyn returned to her bed, not to leave it for some time.

The first day she arose from it, weak, but calm and collected, she said to me, "Now, Mary, you may give me the lock of hair and the miniature, and read me the account of my young hero's death. I can bear all—the worst is past."

Seeing that I still wept, and hesitated to do her bidding, she arose, gently took the keys from my hands, and unlocked the bureau, where unknown to her I had secreted these touching memorials of a happiness now past forever. With a calmness more piteous to behold than any violent grief, she opened all and read all. Then gently clasping her hands, she sank upon her knees, saying, "I was not worthy of him. Thy will be done, oh God! Thy will be done."

CHAPTER XIII.

NAPLES AND THE NEAPOLITANS.

MUCH has been said and written by poets and philosophers on the evanescent nature of all earthly joys, and the precarious tenure on which we hold our happiness here below; but while this is indubitally true, let us be thankful that in the divine decrees of a wise Providence, sorrow is of a nature equally transient. The human heart shrinks from suffering and yearns to be blessed. Such is the unerring law of our being, and He who " tempers the wind to the shorn lamb," mercifully permits Time, that great physician, to pour balm into our deepest wounds, though ever and anon a word, a flower, a perfume, a breath, will cause them to bleed afresh, and throb with exquisite agony.

The night shadow which since the death of Reginald Melville had enveloped our little party, had gradually given place to the aurora of renewed hope.—

Evelyn by degrees regained her health and cheerful spirits, though she ceased not to reproach herself as the involuntary cause of Reginald's death. Ella had become very thoughtful, and appeared to us at times to wander in her mind. She frequently said, " Mama, I saw him last night ; he bid me pray for him."

Or she would chide us for being sad, " He is happy, dearest mama—he told me so."

Once she said with much solemnity, raising her hand as if to impress her words upon our hearts :

" Mother, Reginald bids me tell you he loves you and still watches over you, and you will meet again."

The child frequently spoke of this suddenly, without premeditation, looking up from her book, or her work, or even while nursing her doll. We thought this death had made too deep an impression on her youthful mind, and endeavored as much as possible to divert her thoughts from so melancholy a subject, but we only partially succeeded. She would refer to it again and again, not in sadness, but as if she realized a presence unperceived by others, and was a medium of communication between the land of spirits and the world of sense.

We lived in strict seclusion, our sole distraction being to visit occasionally, in company with a few

friends, the storied and romantic environs of Naples.
The gulf of Salerno, the village of Amalfi, with
its panorama of mountains, the ruins of Paestum,
where the balmy and fragrant breeze is laden with
the baleful breath of fever; and, lastly, Pompeii,
with her numerous villas, where of old the enervated
patricians of ancient Rome enjoyed the *dolce far
niente* of a voluptuous climate, heedless of the fiery
destruction which, at any moment, might over-
whelm their fair town, and hurry those unthinking
votaries of pleasure into eternity. Bulwer's "Last
Days of Pompeii" contains a description so graphic,
and so true of this ill-fated city, that we cannot do
better than refer our readers to that classic work.
We may, however, be permitted to add, that never
before or since has so beautiful a site been chosen
for town or village as was that summer resort of the
Romans. The vistas which opened upon us through
each fluted column, and beneath each sculptured
archway—of the blue Mediterranean—of Vesuvius
and his attendant mountains, their vine-clad val-
leys all colored by the heavenly hues of Southern Italy—Oh! this was a sight which will forever
remain impressed on my senses and on my heart.

The Duc di Balzano—of whom mention has previously been made—was frequently our escort in
these delightful excursions. During Evelyn's illness

and time of trial, he had been untiring in those
attentions which spring from the natural goodness
of the heart. We now considered him quite as a
friend; and never has it been my lot to meet
a more unselfish character. He was a man of much
influence in his native land, and this he always
exerted for the good of others. Nearly connected
by the marriage of a cousin, with the king, his sympathies were royalist and anti-revolutionary; yet he
was kindness itself to the poor and oppressed of his
nation, and had frequently run the risk of compro-
mising himself politically, in order to save those
who had implored his protection, which no one ever
solicited in vain.

About this time, a circumstance occurred which
greatly increased our esteem for one whose nature
was even more noble than his birth, though that
were of the highest in the land. The Duc di Balzano lounged away much of his time at the fashionable *cafés*, which, like our clubs, are with the young
Italians a much-frequented place of rendezvous.
As he was standing in the doorway, Evelyn passed
in her carriage through the Toledo.

I have stated, in a former page, that our heroine
had not altogether escaped the tongue of calumny—
that pale daughter of Envy, engendered by cowardice, and nurtured by hatred and deceit. Evil report

had even pursued her in her solitude ; and now, as she passed, and gracefully acknowledged the respectful salutation of di Balzano, a knot of young exquisites, who only knew her by sight, commenced a conversation, of which the English signora was the subject :

"*E una bella donna*," said the Prince Cassero, "but they say she is the cast off mistress of the Count Syracuse."

"Ah, yes," said another, "and her lover killed himself in despair."

"She is evidently," said a third, "a *donna leggiera*."

"Well," lisped a youth of about seventeen, "she is a fine creature, and sympathetic. I think I shall make her acquaintance."

De Balzano could bear no more ; he sprang into the midst of this dastardly coterie like a tiger. He was superb in his disdainful anger.

"Gentlemen," he said, "you are all cowards. That English lady is my friend, and you shall all answer to me for what you have said, or make a most humble apology in writing, confessing that your statements are false. I expect to hear from you at the Palazzo Balzano."

Thus saying, he left the *café* and returned home. He was a crack shot, fenced beautifully, and was

an adept at the sword exercise. It is, after this, useless to say that a full and ample apology was made
in writing by all the offenders, and from that moment not a whisper was ever breathed against the
fair fame of the English signora.

Too delicate to inform us of this circumstance
himself, we heard of it by chance some days afterwards, through one who had been a spectator of the
scene. Our grateful acknowledgments to our kind
protector may be easily imagined; and from that time
di Balzano became a constant visitor at our home.

We presented our credentials to our kind and
respected minister, Sir W. Temple, who received
us with true English hospitality. Once more we
entered the glittering halls of pleasure — once
more my heroine became apparently the gayest
of the gay; but she had learned a lesson. No
longer a coquette, she sought the society of ladies, rather than that of the opposite sex. Di
Balzano had no reason for jealousy; poor fellow—
I saw that his heart was irretrievably hers. He
paid her the most respectful attention, and she appeared to feel for him sincere friendship and esteem
—nothing more.

Yet such a marriage might have satisfied even
one as fastidious as was Evelyn. Balzano was
handsome, noble, good, independent in fortune,

and deeply in love; he was manly, (a rare quality
in an Italian,) honorable, brave, and unselfish almost to a fault.

But our heroine chose to imagine him unduca-
ted, and not sufficiently *spirituel*. She observed
that after dinner he felt inclined to take a siesta.—
Her old failing of despising a devoted heart, came
back in full force. Was she not beautiful?—had
she not been adored by Melville and others? She
might look higher—if not as to birth, at least as regards intellect. She was not content with plain
common sense in a husband, united with the artistic
taste innate in most of the children of beautiful
Italy. She did not at that time appreciate the inestimable bliss of tranquil domestic life. She would
shine, she would be somebody in the world—the
wife of a Cabinet Minister, of a great general, an
orator, a poet. She desired to queen it, in society;
she was in truth a worldling at heart, a very slave
to the pomps and vanities of life—not perhaps for
their own intrinsic merit, but as a means of gratify-
ing those ambitious desires, which as a vulture de-
voured every good feeling of her nature. But God,
as a tender Father, who chastises but to bless, was
leading her in His own way, and preparing for her
unwilling feet, a path so steep and thorny, that
could the future have been at that time disclosed

to her, she would have shrunk back appalled from its dreariness, and have clung with the tenacious grasp of despair to this her last hope of happiness on earth.

CHAPTER XIV.

"AND so, *bella mia*, I may at last be permitted
to congratulate you on your engagement to the Duc
di Balzano. If I understand aright, he will very
shortly place a coronet on the fair brow he so much
admires—is it not so?"

"Not exactly, Mary," said Evelyn, looking up
from a sketch she was making. "You know, dear,
that Balzano has himself placed a serious impedi-
ment in the way of our marriage. He insists on my
becoming a Catholic."

"I am perfectly aware of that, Evelyn," I answered, "but I thought you were well disposed toward the faith of Rome, and that your present sojourn in this city was with a view to studying the
dogmas of the Catholic Church."

"Precisely so, Mary—and for that reason also,
Balzano has presented to us the chaplain of His

Holiness, Monsignore Dormer, for whose spiritual counsel I am sincerely thankful. Yet I cannot force my conscience, nor be converted against my convictions."

"Pardon me," I rejoined, "but have you not done wrong in raising hopes which may never be realized?"

"Really," replied she, "if the gentleman himself makes these conditions, I do not see how any blame can possibly attach to me."

"You are aware, Evelyn, that the conditions you speak of are rather those of the laws of his country, than his own. As a Protestant, your marriage with a Catholic would in Naples be considered illegal, and your children illegitimate. A dispensation from the Pope would, on the other hand, be too costly. You have therefore no alternative—either you must give up the marriage, or change your religion."

"Oh, you sensible creature!" exclaimed Evelyn, with some petulance. "Miss Edgeworth must have had you as her model when she portrayed her prudent and proper heroines. Why, my dear soul, Catholics never marry in Lent—so I have two months before me—'Sufficient for the day is the evil thereof.'"

"Ah! Evelyn, Evelyn, incorrigible at thirty as at thirteen, when will you come to years of discretion!"

The entrance of di Balzano put an end to our conversation, which took place one evening in our apartment in the Piazza di Spagna, in Rome, where we had ostensibly come with the view of assisting at the ceremonies of the Holy Week. The duke came to propose for that evening a party to view the Coliseum by moonlight. Ever love-loyal to his lady's lightest wish, her lover's one thought was to give her pleasure; and as his friends and acquaintances were all highly placed, we had facilities for sight-seeing rarely granted to strangers.

Our mornings were usually employed in lionizing the various galleries and churches of the Eternal City. To one small chamber in the Vatican we returned again and again. Need I say, it was to pass hours before the most perfect statue ever fashioned by mortal chisel—the glorious, the divine Apollo! Oh! I can well imagine how a young maiden pined away and died for love of that majestic form—those delicate features, so beautiful in their proud consciousness of power. I can well believe how her tender bosom thrilled with a hope that was almost an agony, as she in fancy beheld the magnetic flame of life animate the marble and reveal the present god. Ah, me! poor child—and is she the only one of her sex who has lived, and loved—aye, and died for a shadow—a phantasy? Are we not all doomed to make idols, and, sooner or later, to "find them clay?"

Evelyn and myself agreed that, on leaving these galleries, as it were, "drunk with beauty," every one we met appeared to us plain and homely. Rome is rather unfavorable to the development of the tender passion. Nor did it surprise me that here Numa Pompilius preferred a visionary nymph to a daughter of earth.

Our time passed pleasantly enough; yet Evelyn appeared to suffer from low spirits, and occasionally I surprised her shedding tears. As the chaplain of the Pope came constantly to give her religious instruction, I imagined her mind was influenced by his pious conversation, and deeply desired it might be so, for her future good and that of her daughter. I do not now allude so much to her becoming what it is the fashion in England to call "a Pervert," but to her being seriously and practically convinced, that trust in God, combined with a desire to please Him and to obey His commandments, is the only foundation for true happiness, either here or hereafter. Evelyn being a highly imaginative person, passionately fond of music—in short, an idealist—I considered the Catholic form of worship would be highly attractive to her, and trusted any impression she might now receive would prove lasting.

Nevertheless, I sometimes feared that even the devotion of di Balzano had not met with the return it merited. It appeared to me as if my friend were more influenced by the rank and position of her *fiancé* than by her heart, in the choice she had made. Her own standing in society she had somewhat damaged by past imprudence, and so unexceptionable a marriage was too wise a step to admit of hesitation in a mere worldly point of view. But the evidently deep attachment of Balzano deserved a more worthy return. He was not, it is true, romantic or sentimental; but his heart was noble and affectionate, and he had placed it wholly in the keeping of her he hoped ere long to call his bride. He had no brilliant talent, certes; but he possessed sound common sense and great tact. Young, handsome, aristocratic, a "lion," and unmistakably in love. What could any reasonable woman require more? So thought I, at least; and as I watched the couple, to outward appearance so well matched, I augured for Evelyn a future almost devoid of the clouds which so frequently darken the matrimonial horizon.

Many of the noble ladies of Rome, friends of the duke, took great interest in the probable conversion of his English betrothed ; and books and pamphlets were sent her in abundance by these fair zealots and kindly well-wishers to what they considered a most holy cause

We had, at length, reached that period of the year when the Church of Rome celebrates, with every adjunct of pomp and circumstance, the great mysteries of our redemption. The ladies admitted to view the ceremonies within the railings of the Church of St. Peter must be costumed in black, and wear a black lace mantilla, or veil on their heads, in lieu of a bonnet. The Holy Week commences by the blessing of the Palms, which are afterwards distributed among the people. Each succeeding day has its appropriate services ; and on Holy Thursday, two very grand ceremonies take place— that of washing the feet of twelve old men by His Holinness, in imitation of Jesus washing his apostles' feet ; and next, the great function of the "Cena," or Supper, when these same twelve are served at table by Bishops and Cardinals.

On Easter Sunday, after a magnificent service in the Cathedral, the Pope is carried in a chair to a balcony situated near the roof of the building, and from this fearful elevation he blesses the kneeling multitude congregated in the immense piazza of St. Peters. Pio Nono has a remarkably fine sonorous voice; and, as he spoke the Latin address from that dizzy height, not one syllable was lost.

It was a most imposing and touching sight, that crowd of all nations and all creeds, without distinction of age or sex, all bending in humility to receive the apostolic benediction. Many around had tears in their eyes; nor were my own heretical orbs altogether free from such weakness. A moment, and the clank of arms, the roll of the drums, and the boom of artillery announce the close of the ceremony. We pick ourselves up, stealthily wipe our eyes, enter the carriage, drive to our hotel, and proceed to—luncheon.

"Sic transit gloria mundi."

CHAPTER XV.

IMMEDIATELY subsequent to the conclusion of the ceremonies of the Easter week, Rome is suddenly deserted by the crowd of strangers who have thronged her churches, and elbowed each other in her galleries and palaces. They fly to Naples, Florence, Paris, London, as may be. And yet the environs of the Eternal City are well worth a more than casual visit.

It was now the month of May, and the glowing sun of Italy had already clothed the trees with their spring foliage, and scattered flowers into the lap of Earth. An excursion to the beautiful and romantic grotto of Egeria was planned—and our little party, accompanied by di Balzano, started in the early morning on our expedition. What an apparently happy society !—two lovers, on the eve of a marriage of inclination, a beloved child, a sincere friend, all united for the express purpose of enjoy-

ment. Above us, the purple canopy of an Italian
heaven—around, the varied beauties of scenery
whilst the tepid and perfumed breeze of the South
fanned our cheeks, and breathed new life into our
frames. Surely no element of enjoyment was wanting ; and yet, strange to relate, of all that party Ella alone appeared free from care. Evelyn's attic
brow was clouded, and her eyelids " drooped with
unshed tears." The usually cheerful and light-
hearted Balzano was serious and silent—myself
nervous and restless—for I had a task before me,
which, however unpleasant, I had resolved on performing: it was a duty, and I would not shrink
from it. Thus was our drive any thing but social.

On arriving at the spot where travellers quit their
carriages to walk to the grotto, we alighted—and
after patiently undergoing the usual amount of vic-
timization from those harpies the guides, who remorselessly rob you of your illusions while they
empty your pockets, we succeeded in debarrassing
ourselves of their services on the promise of a second *bottiglia,** on our return to the carriage. We
were thus enabled to wander unmolested through .
the cool and secluded paths in the vicinity of the
fountain and grotto of the nymph. Ella at once

---

* The Italian term for drink-money,

THE GROTTO OF EGERIA.

seized upon her friend Balzano, and insisted that he should take her on an exploring expedition! Evelyn and myself, soon weary with our wanderings, seated ourselves near the moss-clad basin, from which for ever flows the crystal spring, sacred to the mysterious loves of the immortal maiden and her Roman lover.

"I have often wondered," she observed, "whether this legend of ancient Rome is founded on truth, or whether Egeria was but the symbol of the inspired teachings received by Numa in his solitary communings with nature."

"I have always considered this as a myth," I replied. "All the fables of ancient Greece and Rome had some hidden meaning other than a merely sensuous one—and this was probably as you have stated, an allegory."

"And yet," said Evelyn, "it suits my fancy—at least while here—to believe, that all-potent love drew the heaven-born maiden from her solitudes, and that as she pillowed her fair head upon the manly bosom of her human lover, her throbbing heart timidly confessed that even Paradise had for her no higher joy. I believe with Byron, that love is 'no habitant of earth.'"

"Ah! Evelyn," I exclaimed, "*you* at least have no right to say so—for never was mortal woman more truly, more devotedly loved, than you have been, and still are."

"Why not add," said she, smiling sadly, "that never has mortal woman made a more ungrateful return? Granted, dear Mentor—and what then?"

"What then? What a question!—when you are on the eve of marriage with one who possesses almost every quality you can desire. I say *almost*, for perfection is not to be found here below."

Evelyn was silent for a few moments; then rising, she said, as one inspired, her cheek glowing her eyes flashing, while her voice trembled with an emotion to which she rarely gave way—

"Hear me, Mary. Do not think me insensible. The passion so frequently misnamed love on earth is but its counterfeit. Love, as I understand it, is a spiritual passion—a union of souls—that magnetic or electric affinity which is as irresistible as it is indissoluble; for it makes of two imperfect creatures one perfect being—it replaces the original self with another and dearer self; so that where once all thoughts and feelings culminated in the *ego*, they are now centered in *Tu*. This love knows neither change nor death—nor jealousy, strong as death; for it places implicit trust in the beloved one—and if, by chance, that trust is misplaced—ah! then," shuddering, and placing her hand on her bosom—

"then the fountain of life is quenched, and the world say, 'Ah! she died of a broken heart.' But this love," she continued, pointing to heaven, "is there, and there only. While here,

> "'If there be a sympathy in choice,
> War, death, or sickness doth lay siege to it,
> Making it momentary as a sound,
> Swift as a shadow, brief as any dream.

"Such our sad destiny!"

Evelyn paused, and, coming close to me, seated herself; and taking my hand, she said, as her eyes slowly filled with tears: "Poor Balzano! would that he had loved you, Mary. You have more heart to bestow than I have. Mine has depths, few—none may ever sound. And now, tell me, candidly, ought I to marry him?"

She looked anxiously into my face. I scarcely knew what to reply. The strength of her—what shall I say?—imagination surprised me; or rather, are not the mind's ideal shapes more *real* than that which we term reality?

Evelyn withdrew her hand, and turned away disappointed. "I feared you would not understand me," she sighed.

"Yes, dear," I replied. Though your character is a rare one, I can comprehend, and even sympathize with you. Still, it seems to me that you are

wilfully throwing away another chance of happiness
for a chimera—a visionary bliss you can never hope
to realize. You will learn to love Balzano devotedly
when you are once his wife—the angel of the sanc-
tuary of his home."

"Alas! Mary, I shall never—never love him as
I *could*—love, as I *ought* to love a husband. Still,
I have a sincere affection for him, am deeply grateful for his devotion, and value all his noble qualities ; but our souls would forever remain apart. He
could never dwell enshrined within the temple of
my heart. I would give him all in my power to
give. More than that I could not do. Pity me!
for the pain it will cost me to break this off. Indeed,
I dread, above all, not being able to make *him*
happy. Could I do so, if wretched myself?"

"Well, dearest," I said, "if this be so, you must
let him know, without further delay. My intention
was to say this to you to-day; but you have forestalled me. Let me, however, entreat you to consider well—the time may come when you will, perhaps, deeply regret having rejected so honorable
and noble a heart, for a caprice, a fancy.

"Alas!" she rejoined, bitterly—"I feel that,
whether I unite my fate with the noble Balzano, or
whether I decide to remain alone and unloved, re-

gret will equally be mine. Such is my cruel destiny!"

Just then we heard Ella's ringing laugh, and rose to meet them.

On leaving the grotto, we perceived Balzano; his hat, his pockets, his hands, all crammed with wild flowers and mosses for his pet's herbarium. As I looked on his fine open countenance, beaming with good nature, and now animated with the pleasure of amusing a child, I almost wondered at Evelyn's insensibility, even admitting he was no type of that spiritual beauty she had taken as her *beau ideal*.

During our drive homeward, it struck me that Evelyn's manner was softer and kinder towards her lover than it had been for some time. Did she relent? or was it the tender pity a woman ever feels toward a suitor she is determined to reject, knowing at the same time she is fondly loved?

We retired early to rest; but, before we parted for the night, I received Evelyn's promise that she would, on the following morning, enter into a full explanation with her betrothed. Of the particulars of that conversation I was made aware later.

Punctually at twelve, to the minute, as per agreement, the duke entered our *salon*. Evelyn was alone. She was very pale, but calm and collected.

" *Mon ami*," she began, " I wish to speak to you very seriously."

" Why so, *anima mia?*" (my soul)—taking her hand, and dropping on one knee, as he gallantly raised the jeweled fingers to his lips—" why should we be serious, when everything smiles on our projected union?"

" Hush, Balzano!" she replied, gently withdrawing her hand, and motioning him to a chair. " Listen to me for one moment. It is important to our happiness—indeed it is."

Her solemn manner alarmed him; for the ready tear stood in his dark eyes, and he said sadly :

" I see it all—you do not love me!"

" Yes, dear friend—indeed—indeed I do. I think no one so good, so noble, so devoted as you."

"Then what is it, *cuore mio?*" (my heart)— " speak."

"I cannot!" said Evelyn, blushing, and not daring to look her lover in the face—for she knew that she was deceiving him—" the fact is, I cannot be a Catholic just yet; I should not like to confess."

"If that is all, lady mine," said Balzano, again smiling, " it can soon be arranged. Indeed, what sins shall you have to confess, unless, perhaps," and he laughed—his old gay laugh—" you intend to like some one better than your husband ? "

"Dear Balzano, forgive me, and let me have my own way this once—return to Naples, and let me go to Paris. I can profess Catholicism there; and besides, that is the only place where your bride could get the elegant *toilette* she will require to do you honor. Remember, Signor Duca, I shall be a Duchess."

"Take your own way, my only beloved; I will do as you bid me. But, ah! I dread leaving you—I have a presentiment of evil."

He flung himself on his knees before her; and they mingled sobs and tears. How long they remained thus, Evelyn never knew. She only felt him strain her for a moment to his breast, imprint a kiss on her brow, and then he was gone; the door closed on the manly form, and the light of the kind and loving face no longer beamed upon her.

They never met on earth again.

CHAPTER XVI

ROSSINI.

THEY never met on earth again. In this world where all is uncertain, how terrible are partings! Which of us can utter that fatal word, farewell, and not feel a thrill through the heart of indistinct terror — a vague *perhaps*, which will whisper, who knows but that mine eyes have mirrored for the last time that familiar face, that loved form! that mine ears have drank in for the last time the music of that gentle voice! It is fearful on what "trifles light as air," hang the destiny of a life. A glance, a word misconstrued, may forever separate those who till then, were fast friends; forever banish them from out of our life. To those who have not the consoling hope of immortality in a brighter sphere, what a tangled, hopeless wilderness, must this world appear. And yet we live on; we dress, and smile, and mix with the crowd; we hide the never satisfied yearnings of our hearts beneath the rich tissues of lace and satin, and compress the sighs of the weary bosom with bands of diamonds and pearls. Such is life.

We had now been some time in Paris—that city of fashion—where not to be *bien habillé* is a mortal sin. There neither beauty nor talent avail with a woman unless her *chapeau* be from Laure or Baudreant, and her *robe* modelled in the *atelier* of Roger or Delphine. If in addition, she be handsome and agreeable, so much the better; but even then, the first salutation would certainly be from ladies, and very probably from the sterner sex, " *Oh, Madame, que vous êtes élégante vous avez vraiment une toilette délicieuse.*"

Evelyn and myself, with Ella, who was now growing up, used occasionally to spend our evenings in the *salon* of Rossini, to whom we had been presented in Florence, and who was now settled in a magnificent apartment in the Chausseé d'Antin. Here we met, from time to time, all the celebrities of the artistic world, whether of music, painting or the dance; also the leading journalists and musical critics of the day, with an occasional sprinkling of the *beau monde.*

Rossini, at first sight, does not impose upon the mind as the greatest musical genius of his age, and one of the first of any era. You behold a simple

old man, somewhat portly, with a face remarkable
for its *bonhomie*. The features fine, forehead high
and intellectual, surmounted by, I regret to say, a
very ugly wig of reddish brown; withall, a fresh,
but not red complexion, of which any much younger
man might be proud. He looks a dear, benevolent
old man, who would greatly enjoy a good dinner,
and this, in fact, is the case. Such would be a first
sight judgment, but a better acquaintance would
show that the benign countenance could light up
with the *sourire fin* and the *malice* we should expect to find in the author of the first and best of
musical comedies—the ever fresh, the peerless, the
immortal "Barbiere di Seviglia." Rossini has acquired the reputation of being very satirical—ill-
naturedly so. Yet it is not the case, for true mod-
esty, combined with real talent, could never meet
with a kinder, more generous, or more indulgent
critic than in him. Unhappily, however, the *salon*
of Rossini is besieged by a crowd of know-nothings
who imagine that to display their médiocre acquire-
ments before this great man, is to partake in some
measure of his genius. Poor fools! if they had only
seen, as I have, the persecuted composer rub-
bing his head, (a habit with him when annoyed), till
his very wig was actually turned hind before, from
sheer nervous excitement, I think, I say, had they

beheld this, even shrill sopranos and roaring bari-
tones, would have ceased in pity from the remorse-
less murders they were perpetrating upon the dear
children of his brain. Once I remember, when a
cruel lady had worried him past bearing, and adding insult to injury, had changed almost every note
in his aria, and worse than all, expected a compliment from her victim, the *maestro* advanced to
the piano, and said in his mild, soft voice, "Pray,
madame, who is the composer of that music?"

On another occasion he observed to a prima donna, whose singing was more remarkable for execu-
tion than expression, "Madame, you sing with wonderful *agilité;* you are rapid as a railway train, but
you know I am afraid of railways."

Here let me remark that Rossini's cowardice is
great as his genius. He fears everything—railways,
the sea, illness; more than all, death. The idea of
the latter appears to embitter all his life; it is the

"One shadow that throws,
Its bleak shade alike o'er his joys and his woes."

He has no religious belief—no hope which divests
the grave of its terrors. Rossini confesses to being
a coward, and often turns the laugh against himself.
I remember with what humor he once recounted to

us an incident of his early youth. He was at Naples during one of its many political convulsions,
and was, much to his disgust, made a "garde Na-
tionale," and, of course, expected to take turns of
duty with the others. The young musician excused
himself on the plea of his well-known want of courage. His excuse, however, was not accepted. Poor
Gioacchino was equipped *en militaire*, furnished
with a musket, and ordered into the sentry-box to
keep guard.

"I entered," said Rossini, "and remained there
about an hour, trembling in every limb. At last I
heard, or thought I heard, footsteps. I laid down
my musket gently, and slipped out of my *guérite*,
and then I ran as fast as my legs could carry me,
and never stopped till I reached home and was safe
under the blankets in my bed. In the morning they
put me under arrest, and would have shot me.—
But," added Rossini, with evident pride, "I escaped
because I was the author of 'Il Barbiere.'"

The father of the young genius was by no means
remarkable for musical talent. He used to play the
horn in the orchestra conducted by his son. One
day Papa played too outrageously false to escape
censure.

"Who is that bad horn?" said young Rossini, pre-
tending ignorance.

"It is I, my son," said Rossini *père*.

"Then, papa, I am sorry, but you must leave the orchestra."

One more *bon mot* I must mention. One evening, on our return from the performance of "La Gazza Ladra," at the Italian Opera, we went to pay a visit to the *Maestro*. Rossini manifested the most perfect indifference as regarded the vocalists, but made anxious enquiries as to the way in which the magpie had performed her part. Many other anecdotes might be recounted, but here we can give but a passing notice of this wonderful man —wonderful in his greatness, and scarcely less so in his weaknesses. Usually silent in general society, it is in a *tête-à-tête* with a sympathetic companion, that Rossini betrays the versatility of his genius and the extent of his information. He appears conversant with all subjects. Notwithstanding the rich vein of humor which sparkles in his music and in his conversation, Rossini, like Byron, is a melancholy man. Nor is this singular, for I have invariably found that the wittiest and most *spirituel* are ever the saddest; and those who press to their lips with the keenest relish the cup of pleasure, when the moments of excitement and intoxication are over, too frequently drain to the very dregs the chalice of misery.

Rossini was much attached to Evelyn, her remarkable musical talents and profound worship of his genius, made them a most happy pair of friends. On her acquainting him with her possible marriage with the Duc di Balzano, "My child," replied the old man, "Never marry except for one of three things: a great name, a great talent, or a large fortune."

'Tis true for him matrimony had offered but few attractions. From his first wife—Madame Colbran —a singer of undoubted talent, the *maestro* was soon separated. As to the second, let us respect her name, she is yet living, but I fear she conduces little to the domestic comfort of her lord. It is remarkable how few celebrities of either sex have been happy in their affections. Commencing with Socrates and his Xantippe, we may cite Milton, Shakespeare, Byron, Dante, Tasso, Goethe, Mrs. Hemans, Mrs. Norton, and a crowd of others, all mis-matched or crossed in love, while Mr. and Mrs. Jones, and Tom Smith and wife, with A and B, and numerous other worthies, whose thoughts are centred in pounds or dollars, as may be, and their multiplied progeny, are perfectly content. Is it that they have bodies but no souls to satisfy? or doth God when he confers on his children the divine gift of creative power, ever twine with thorns the laurel wreath

which encircles their noble brow, baptizing them for
His own with the drops of agony wrung from their
hearts? So thought and so feared our heroine, and
Rossini confirmed her in her resolve to preserve her
liberty for the present.

Evelyn had continued to correspond with Balzano, but still repudiated the idea of marriage on the
plea that she could not at present conscientiously
change her belief. The latter, after some months,
became, very naturally, anxious that his ladye-love
should come to some decision, and to enable her
to do so, he consented, he said, to her remaining a
Protestant, and would, on receiving her reply, at
once exert his interest to get a dispensation from the
Pope. Thus was my fair friend obliged at last
either to accept the love of one to whom she felt
unable to give her whole heart, or to lose the friendship, perhaps forever, of the man she esteemed most
on earth—a common but not the less an unpleasant
dilemma. Well, what did she do? Why, she put
off answering the letter as long as she could; asked
the advice of all her friends on a point on which she
alone could judge; and after having consulted
every one was as far from a decision as ever.

Evelyn, like all very impressionable people, was
apt to be greatly influenced by her surroundings; yet
was she not inconstant. She would forget, for the

moment, and appear to be utterly free from all thought of the absent; but the excitement past, she would return with deeper passion to the memories of by-gone days. As yet, no one had approached Balzano in her heart. He still reigned alone—manly, noble, tender, the kind protector, the devoted friend; and yet she hesitated to make him happy, and, I must add, to be happy herself—for what woman could be otherwise with such a man?

Another letter, still more pressing, came from the now anxious lover. Was his friend sick? in trouble? She was but to say one word. He would fly to her—to her he must love till the pulses of life ceased to beat—his bride, his soul, his delight.

I found Evelyn in tears, with the open letter in her hand. "I will certainly write to-morrow," she said.

CHAPTER XVII.

THE to-morrow of our good intentions, sometimes, it may be frequently, never dawns. On this particular to-morrow, according to Parisian custom, we were to be at home to our friends.

Our morning was devoted to the duties of the toilet and those of the *ménage*. There was a duett to be practiced for piano and harp by myself and Ella, who now played that graceful instrument with exquisite taste. She was also to accompany her mother on the harp, in the lovely romance and prayer from Rossini's Otello, by particular request of the *Maestro* himself. Evelyn received well. Her *salon* was much frequented by *artistes* and men of letters; and a few charming female friends added greatly to the brilliancy of these réunions.

A thorough musician herself, she had a perfect horror of the usual style of amateur singing; and no one was permitted, at her house, to display their

7

mediocrity at the expense of the nerves of the company.

Our apartment was situate in the Avenue Gabriel —to my taste, the most delightful location in Paris. Near, yet not actually in, the Champs Elysées, it combines cheerfulness and gaiety with privacy and retirement. Our apartment was *au rez de chaussée* (on the ground floor), all the rooms, as is usual in Paris, *en suite.* It had been furnished with remarkable taste by a Russian Princess, who, being suddenly recalled by the Czar, was glad to let her apartment to English ladies—on, to us, most advantageous terms. We were, therefore, lodged as few strangers may hope to be. The suite of rooms were now thrown open, and brilliantly lighted—all except Evelyn's boudoir, which led into the conservatory, and in which reigned a subdued light, inviting to lovers or to those who prefer to muse in solitude and watch the crowd from afar. At present, all were congregated in the *salon,* around the fair hostess, who herself looked like a queen surrounded by her court.

" *Ah ! ma chère,*" exclaimed a pretty vivacious little marquise, perfumed like a rose, as only a French woman can be—" your *soirée* is really charming— delicious—but pardon me, there are two things, or rather persons, wanting to make your réunion perfect."

"Indeed," replied Evelyn, smiling; "and pray, who may these be?"

"Nay, you must guess," rejoined another fair lady of the party; "for, at present, those two persons are indispensible in the *beau monde*."

"Perhaps," suggested Evelyn, "you mean my dear friend Rossini?"

"Oh! no; we are all aware he is quite a hermit."

"The Emperor, perhaps, and the peerless Castiglione?"

"Neither, I assure you," persisted the pretty marquise.

"Well, Wagner, the 'musician of the future.'"

"Madame, you surprise me," said a beautiful Spanish countess, advancing into the circle—"you a *dame du grand monde*, and not to have heard of the great magician *par exemple!*"

"And who, pray, may that be, countess?"

"Oh!" drawled an Englishman, "the man who calls up the devil, and made Napoleon come out of his tomb and sign his name, or something of that sort."

"And," added another, "frightened poor Eugenie out of her wits."

"No very difficult matter, either," growled an old

legitimist with a brown wig, " considering how few wits she has, if report speak true."

" *Fi donc, monsieur*," or " not so bad," chimed in the audience at this rather obvious *witticism* in every sense.

" I suppose," said Evelyn " you mean Home, the Medium. We are, I believe, to meet him next week. So your swan, Madame la Marquise, has turned out to be a goose, after all. And now for that other, without whom no party is complete."

" That, madame," said a young Frenchman, full of conceit and affectation, " is a long-bony American, about whom, it appears, all the ladies are raving— though, *ma foi*, I cannot imagine what for, except that they say he is enormously rich."

" Precisely so," said the perfumed little marquise, "but monsieur is jealous, for my Yankee *is* very handsome, but disdainful, *à briser le coeur*—Monsieur D'Arcy."

" D'Arcy," exclaimed Evelyn, " I expect him here to-night. Madame de Villiers has requested permission to present him, and——"

At this moment the folding doors were thrown open, and a charming and aristocratic looking elderly lady, richly but simply attired, entered leaning on the arm of a gentleman, whom she presented with much *empressement* to the lady of the house.

"Talk of his Satanic Majesty," whispered the Englishman, while a smile might be perceived on more than one pair of rosy lips, as the unconscious object of all this *persiflage* advanced into the charmed circle and gracefully paid his *devoirs* to its presiding genius.

Philip D'Arcy was one of those rarely endowed beings who, at first sight, impress you with a sense of power—you feel you are in the presence of one born to command. Where this moral force is combined with magnetic influence, or odic affinity, if you please so to term that irresistible attraction we all have felt, more or less at times, then the fascination of such a being is irresistible. He can draw you according to the degree of your sensitive nature, into his sphere, as into a vortex. Nor can you escape. —Fatal gift, if dissevered from heart and principle!

Mr. D'Arcy may have been about thirty ; slightly above the medium stature, his erect and lofty bearing gave the idea of greater height than he actually possessed. But for this too—the extreme delicacy of his form, (a defect common to the transatlantic race of the Northern States), might perhaps, have been considered as somewhat detracting from the manliness of his appearance. To say that the features were chiselled, were little. Intellect sat enthroned on the regal brow, and the deep set eyes

—calm, blue, and unfathomable as the ocean—
seemed the fitting mirror of "the human soul divine." The lips firmly closed, pale, and somewhat
severe in their habitual expression, could, nevertheless, occasionally wear a smile of rare beauty. The
complexion, white as Parian marble, harmonized
well with the crisply curling locks, and the full
beard, of that cold, brown tint, which almost uni-
versally accompanies the refined style of male beauty. Mr. D'Arcy engaged Evelyn in that light conversation which, *well talked*, has so much charm,
and beneath which occasionally runs a vein of the
deepest sentiment or the richest humor. But the
tête-à-tête was not of long duration.

Most pressing entreaties drew our heroine to the
harp, before which Ella was seated, having already
commenced the exquisite accompaniment which
preludes the "willow song" of the gentle Desdemo-
na. Ella was now in her fifteenth year. The warm
sun of Italy had almost visibly ripened the child of
a year since into premature womanhood. Though
of a form so slight as to appear almost etherial, she
was already taller than her mother, and so pure was
her girlish beauty, so infantine her air of candid in-
nocence, you might have fancied her the youngest
and loveliest of the nymphs of Diana. Her small,
Grecian head seemed actually bending under the

weight of the rich masses of soft, blond hair, which formed a triple crown above the classic brow, and fastened in a knot behind, fell in a luxuriance of clustering curls to the slender throat.

Though like in feature, Ella formed a striking contrast to her mother; and for the first time I confessed that it were difficult to decide which might bear the palm, the dazzling beauty and ever-varying expression of the still young matron, or the timid, retiring loveliness of the girl. The one appeared as a royal rose, in all her splendor; the other, a tender bud, shrinking even from the kiss of the sunbeam—the former, a gorgeous tropical plant, whose rare beauty can only be equalled by its fragrance; the latter, a sweet and modest lily, hiding amid its leaves in the greenest and most sequestered dell, haunted alone by fairy footsteps.

Evelyn had never sung so well. The rich tones of her voice vibrated with sentiment, as she portrayed the sorrows of the loving but forsaken wife. The audience forgot to applaud, (the greatest compliment that can be paid to a singer.) The lovely minstrel's own eyes were humid with emotion. Ella looked a coldness she perhaps did not feel. Mr. D'Arcy advanced to the harp.

"Madame," he said, "compliment to *you* would be misplaced. The genius of Rossini has found in your own a worthy interpreter. You have sang as he must have desired in his moments of deepest inspiration—when the ideal descending embraced the real. Nay,"—as she prepared to disclaim the praise so delicious to a true artiste, from one whose taste and judgment is felt to be unimpeachable—" nay, fairest songstress,"—and he smiled that smile of rare fascination which thrilled to the very inmost of her being—" if I have praised, it is because I have felt the pathos of those sympathetic tones, the poetry breathing through each phrase of melody, and I," he added, as if to himself, " so rarely indulge in the luxury of emotion. But pray, Mrs. Travers, present me to the young lady who has so ably seconded you."

"To my daughter? Certainly—she is but a child. Ella, dearest, Mr. D'Arcy would make your acquaintance."

The young girl bent to the salutation of the stranger, and a blush of the softest pink overspread features, throat and arms, reaching even to the ends of the taper fingers, as she timidly replied in monosyllables to the few words of common-place civility he addressed to her.

CHAPTER XVIII.

A SERIOUS CHAPTER.

ONE morning about a fortnight after Evelyn's last evening reception, Mr. D'Arcy was announced.

"I take the liberty," said he, "of intruding on a day that I know you are not at home to all the world, in the hope of escaping the usual *toilette* talk at ladies' receptions."

"We are happy to see you, on your own terms, Mr. D'Arcy—the more so, as the part of the hostess is rather an ungrateful one. She is forced to converse *chiffons*, and other frivolities, when she would perhaps prefer to philosophize, if ladies ever dare appear so blue."

"It is for this," replied he, "that I dislike lady's '*days*.' One can never approach the mistress of the house herself, except to make some commonplace observation about the weather, the opera, the 'première réprésentation' at the Varietés — *qui sait ?*" with a French shrug of the shoulders.

7*

"Oh, Mr. D'Arcy, in pity do not imitate the French at my house," exclaimed Evelyn. "If you only knew how their manners—half-monkey, half-hairdresser—annoy me."

"Madame, I stand rebuked," with a mock respectful bow; "but seriously, though it is treason to say it in so fairy-like a bower, my visit to-day is rather on business than pleasure. I come as ambassador from Mme. de Villiers to endeavor to persuade you, ladies, to come to her this evening, and meet Home, the wonder-working medium, about whom all Paris is talking."

"Forestalled," exclaimed Evelyn, gaily; "we were initiated yesterday into some of these weird doings, at the house of an English lady."

"Indeed," said D'Arcy, with evident interest—"and what, may I ask, did you witness?"

"Well, we placed ourselves in a circle of about nine persons, and in a few minutes we heard raps; by the alphabet, we were requested to remove the lights, and after we had done so, an accordeon, which was lying on the table, 'discoursed most excellent music,' *no one touching it.* Then, by the dim light, we perceived a hand, white and beautifully formed—and this hand presented me with a real geranium, and others of the circle with different flowers."

"You are, then, favorably disposed toward the subject of spiritualism?" enquired D'Arcy.

"All I saw has deeply impressed me," replied Evelyn; "and I cannot think it altogether a delusion, for I distinctly felt in my fingers the vibration of the table before each rap, and frequently knew the answer about to be made by the (so-called) spirits, to questions asked by members of the circle."

"Ah! then you must yourself be a medium?"

"Delightful! There is nothing I should like better. You must explain to us these mysteries, and convert my friend there also, for she is a sad infidel."

"I suppose," I rejoined, "I am too matter-of-fact, and have too little imagination to be caught by what I cannot but consider as a mere trick to amuse children, and utterly unworthy rational beings, whether in or out of the body."

"Pardon me, Miss Mildmay," said D'Arcy, "but if these knockings, which appear to you so puerile, have been tested and proved *not* to be tricks, and that such and similar manifestations have been the means of convincing the confirmed sceptic that there is an actual hereafter, it appears to me that the spirits of the departed are rather occupied in a good work, and that *we* have at least 'method in our madness.'"

"But," I answered, "surely the Bible is all-sufficient for the salvation of the world."

"No one, my dear Miss Mildmay," replied D'Arcy, "reveres the Bible more than myself—yet I am bound to confess it never convinced me. Till my eyes were opened to the perception that spirit really *does* exist, palpably, apart from matter, the Bible was to me as a sealed book. In earlier youth, I worshipped as my deity the intellect of man, smiling in contempt at the idea of a blind faith in the mysteries of Religion, which I looked upon as the foolish inventions of a venal and ignorant priesthood. It was through the much despised manifestations of the spirit circle, that I first realized the '*certain hope* of a blessed immortality,' and learned to bow my reason before the Divine inspirations—in fine, *I believed.*"

D'Arcy spoke with the deepest feeling, but calmly, and as a man whose doubts were for ever at rest. You recognized in each word the power of a great mind, and instead of wishing to cavil, you felt your place was rather to sit at his feet and learn.

"One question I would ask," said Evelyn.— "Might not these phenomena be produced by magnetic influence, and so be accounted for in a merely natural way ?"

"Undoubtedly, Mrs. Travers. Human magnetism and the will-power are almost omnipotent as physical forces, and also as influencing the mental faculties ; but the communications being not only intelligent, but actually and frequently even contrary to the desires and expectations of the circle, precludes the idea of entirely accounting for them in the way you have very plausibly suggested. Besides, the phenomena of direct writing and drawing could be explained by no other theory than that of supernatural intervention. Electric shocks, too, have been sensibly felt, and exquisite odours have filled the room—and this in the presence of witnesses, many of them men of superior learning, intelligence, and undoubted piety, who would not for worlds have been made the instruments of propagating fraudulent or erroneous doctrines."

"If you have personally witnessed all you speak of," I said, "I confess that even my incredulity must at last give way before such evidence."

"Gently, Miss Mildmay," interposed D'Arcy. "I desire that each and every one may see and judge for themselves, feeling convinced that no person of average mental powers, having investigated the subject fairly and with candor, could continue a sceptic. To assist you, however, in your research, let me recommend to your notice ' Owen's Footfalls on the Boundaries of Another World.' Likewise the works of Andrew Jackson Davis. Also, the ' Arcana of Christianity,' by the Rev. T. L. Harris, and the eloquent and spiritual discourses of the latter author; lastly, a gem of beauty, a perfect string of pearls, the ' Foregleams of Immortality,' by Sears. This latter work, with those of Mr. Harris, are written in the very spirit of true Biblical and catholic Christianity, untrammelled by the narrow-mindedness of sectarianism. Read these books, not forgetting to breathe a prayer for light, attend some circles, and I think in six months from this time you will tell me that you are really ' born again, and a new creature,' so different will be your views of the infinite destinies of the divine human spirit—so shadowy will appear the present, so real, so near the future."

I looked at him, struck with the intenseness of his manner—his large, blue, serious eyes, filled with the far-off look, of those whose spirits live in perpetual communion with the inner world. Like Ananias, it appeared to me that scales fell from the eyes of my soul, and I began to see things for the first time in their true light. Evelyn also was deeply impressed; after a pause of emotion, she was the first to break silence.

"May I ask," she said, "what first induced you, with your manly intellect and infidel sympathies, to take sufficient interest in this subject to attend a circle?—for if I judge you aright, curiosity alone would scarcely have drawn you there."

"You have justly divined, Mrs. Travers, and I will tell you all."

He paused, and then resumed with deep and touching emotion—

"A young girl, whom I loved, God knows how fondly, was taken from me in the bloom of youth, and on the eve of marriage, by a fearful accident, which left her not a vestige of beauty—burned to death," he said, with a shudder. "A confirmed infidel, with no hope—crushed, tortured, maddened by the idea that she was lost to me forever, I cursed my cruel fate, and should have put an end to a hateful existence, had not pride whispered, 'Do not be mastered by your destiny; conquer it—live.' And I lived. At this time, I heard much of the Miss Foxes, and of the wonderful things occurring in their presence. An impression I could not shake off led me to their house. In bitter mockery, I asked myself, Am I insane? I went to scoff—be it said—but returned to pray. A communication

came thus by raps—'Do not mourn for me, Philip.
I am happy now. I was taken from you, because
you enveloped your soul in pride as in a mantle.
Dear Philip! you must become as a little child.

" ' LILIAN.'

"Imagine my surprise; for I was in a strange
city, where none knew me. I am not ashamed to confess, that tears, foreign to my nature, came unbidden
to my eyes, and the prayer arose to my lips—
'Teach me the truth, Oh! God.' That prayer, dear
friends, has been answered. Since that time I have
been happy ; for I now look at this life in the light
of the other."

"'Tis a beautiful faith," said Evelyn, "that our
loved ones are still about our path—our guardian
angels, perhaps."

"It is a faith I would not lose," said D'Arcy,
"for worlds of untold wealth."

He drew from his neck a delicate hair chain,
with a locket attached. Touching a spring, we
peceived the miniature of a beautiful young girl.
"That portrait," said D'Arcy, "was painted by a
spirit medium, after my Lilian had passed away—it
is her very self—but spiritualized."

"How exquisitely lovely!" I exclaimed.

"Heavens! how like Ella!" cried Evelyn.

CHAPTER XIX

LEAVES FROM A LADY'S DIARY.

March 13*th.*—I have, of late, greatly neglected my journal, not from want of time, neither for lack of incident nor material for thought and feeling— rather the reverse.

Since my last musical reception, I have not penned one line. Oh! that night is a kind of era in my life. I then made the acquaintance of a remarkable man—perhaps *the* most uncommon person I ever met. It is not only that he is very, very handsome, nor highly intellectual, nor most refined in manners—it is that, over and above all these qualifications, he possesses, in a wonderful degree, the power of attraction—magnetism, if you will—the *je ne sais quoi* of the French. You forget self in his presence, and think of him only. I cannot analyze my feelings. I only know, that, as the soft and musical tones of that voice fell on my ear, as I felt the magic of that glance in my inmost soul, the words uttered by Lady Caroline Lamb, when first she beheld Byron, came unbidden to my memory, and seemed to me as a foreboding of sorrow—

> "That pale face is my fate!"

I murmured, as a vague terror crept over me.

On the morning we received Mr. D'Arcy's first visit—Mary and myself—our conversation turned upon spiritual manifestations. I sat and listened—for my own experience and the clairvoyant powers of Ella had long since set me wondering. D'Arcy, it appears, is a firm believer. He recounted to us the circumstances which led to his conversion. Lilian—what a sweet name! Ah! instead of pitying, I almost envied her. Did *he* not say that he had loved her fondly—that he still wore her miniature next his heart? Happy Lilian! Would I could change with thee—to have drained the cup of intoxicating bliss to the dregs, and then to die, to pass away in the freshness of youth—hopes undeceived—trust unshaken—loving, beloved, regretted, happy Lilian! See the reverse, fair spirit, and pity poor Evelyn's far sadder fate! Behold her as the wretched wife of one totally unsuited to her—then, as the murderess of the noble, the loving Reginald—lastly, as the faithless betrothed of the generous-hearted Balzano; and wherefore? Because she is not of the happy "few, who find what they love or could have loved," and who, therefore, are influenced through life by "accident, blind contact, and the *strong necessity of loving*,"—that touchstone of woman's weakness and folly.

21st.—My Ella's birthday. She is now fifteen, and in the eyes of a partial mother, the loveliest of God's feminine creation. Mr. D'Arcy brought her a bouquet of the most priceless hot-house flowers of the purest white—emblematic, he said, of her etherial nature. How good of him to think of her. Though but a child, she doubtless reminds him of his Lilian. I have observed those limpid and unfathomable eyes of his fixed upon her more than once in silent contemplation. He is now a frequent visitor—perhaps *too* frequent. There are flowers so fair, fruits so tempting, that we forget the danger which lurks within. We inhale their perfume; we press to our lips their luscious juice, and *we perish*.

31st.—The first mild day of spring. The air from the conservatory enters laden with the breath of flowers. I feel the blood pulsating in my veins with unusual ardor. There is a bouquet of Parma violets by my side, sent by *him*. Their perfume inebriates my senses; an indefinable charm pene-

trates my whole being. If, after all, he loves me !
Oh! hush! foolish heart be still. Such happiness
is not for earth. And yet, I think he is not indifferent. Friendship from him is preferable to love
from another—yes, it would content me. But then,
friends part, to meet again God alone knows *when*.
This is terrible; and what is friendship when love
intervenes, for another. Oh! that thought is torture. Why, what an ingenious self-tormentor am I.
Why search the possible future to embitter the happy reality of the present. If the worst comes I can
die—no, WE CANNOT DIE, we live ; live forever with
an eternal passion in the heart, when we make of a
mere mortal the "god of our idolatry."

April 15*th*.—This evening, it being my reception
day, and a few intimates having collected in our
salon, the conversation turned upon love and jealousy.

"I cannot," observed D'Arcy, "understand the
simultaneous existence of these two passions in one
bosom."

"How," cried one of the party, "has not jealousy
been termed the 'child of insatiate love?' "

"Nay, rather," rejoined D'Arcy, "has not Tennyson more aptly described this passion as 'dead

love's harsh heir jealous pride.' Where true love exists, believe me, there can be no jealousy."

"Ah!" I exclaimed, and I felt the warm blood mount to my temples, "Mr. D'Arcy is right. True love must be based on esteem, and cannot, therefore, live without perfect confidence."

" You have divined me," said D'Arcy, with that smile of rare sweetness peculiar to him; "jealousy originates in mistrust, and is, therefore, an insult when unfounded."

" But supposing you had cause," said another of the circle.

" Then," replied he, with an almost stern severity, " I should no longer love."

"Ah! ah! monsieur," said a pretty little French-woman, " I differ, quite. As for me, I am jealous; as a wolf—a tiger."

A general laugh followed this innocent and truly French sally, from all but D'Arcy, who bowing profoundly, and with an air of inimitable mock humility, said :

" Then, madame, I am most unhappy, for I can never make love to you."

"This is growing too serious," I said; "let me introduce to you, Mr. D'Arcy, as a poet, and my friend, Miss Mildmay, as a musician second only to

Rossini. Ella will sing you a song of their joint composition. It is really charming."

I here transcribe the words, which, with the music, met with great success :

THE SPIRIT OF LOVE.

My spirit dwelleth in myrtle bowers,
Where the breezes wax faint with the perfume of flowers,
And the queen rose blushes a brighter hue,
As I shed o'er her leaves, the early dew.
On a sunbeam I sit enthron'd in light,
And chase with my wand the shades of night,
And oft beneath the moon's pale beam
I weave with sweet fancies the maiden's dream.

Deep in the woods, the nightingale
Telleth to me her love-lorn tale;
With the glorious lark, I soar on high
As her thrilling notes ring thro' earth and sky.
I love to skim o'er the pathless seas,
Syren-like, singing sweet melodies,
And the home-sick mariner feels my power
In the loneliness of that star-lit hour.

But, oh ! far more do I love to sip
The fragrant dew on beauty's lip,
To braid each tress of her wavy hair,
And tinge with bright blushes her cheek so fair :
O'er the poet's couch my spirit bendeth,
And my form with his visions softly blendeth,
While he whose soul sweet music fires
I glad with the strains of the seraph choirs.

April 27th.—The old adage, "Love is blind," is by no means true, at least in my case. Cupid for me never fails to put on a pair of magnifying glasses, which have the power of exaggerating alike the virtues and defects of those who have with me entered the lists of the tournament of love. I have detested many an admirer for "trifles light as air," cruelly criticising his dress, voice, manner, or tastes ; and I once took a fancy to a person, mainly because his gloves fitted exquisitely—and had the other qualities corresponded, my fancy would, doubtless, have taken other shape. But, to return. To what a severe scrutiny have I not subjected Philip D'Arcy ; but, "alas ! and well-a-day," I find no fault in him. Men frequently term him effeminate-looking ; and it is true, that he is formed in a delicate, rather than a robust mould ; but this suits well with that spiritual style of beauty so preeminent in him : and who could fail to read in the *pose* of that noble head, in the expression of the compressed and chiselled lips, moral grandeur, indomitable will. Women, too, frequently call him cold. Ah ! they have not marked, as I have, that glance of flame which (rarely, it is true) flashes from the depth of those orbs, usually so serene, so untroubled. The volcano may be smouldering, but

it is not extinct. Long years of self-control may
have schooled the heart; but its pulses, nevertheless, throb warmly, passionately, humanly, still.

May 8th.—Mr. D'Arcy possesses, in a remarkable degree, the power of affecting the heart and
imagination with what remains unspoken.   He
sets you thinking.   In his presence, you brush
the rust from your mind, and new ideas flow in
upon you.   To-day, he spoke to us of Swedenborg,
and of the charming and consoling doctrine of that
great Christian seer; that however lonely our earthly
lot, however mistaken we may have been in our
choice of a mate, those who by perseverance in
well doing eventually become angels, will, sooner
or later, meet with their true conjugal partner—
their other self—in a higher sphere.   A beautiful
philosophy, and not unreasonable, when we consider that love, in its true sense, is the strongest and
purest, as well as the most exquisitely delightful
sentiment of our nature : nor would the Creator have
implanted this passion in our souls, but that He intended to satisfy it to the full ; if, therefore, sad
experience shows how rarely on earth we are truly
mated, it follows, logically, that this sweetest and
tenderest of the spirit's yearnings looks for realiza-
tion in a higher sphere of being.   Such, at least, is

D'Arcy's firm belief; such also, he tells me, is that of many of the most eminently intellectual and spiritual of his countrymen and countrywomen. Mary is, of course, charmed: she says there is, at last, some chance for her.

8

CHAPTER XX.

IT was now the middle of summer, and remarkably hot for the season. All our friends had left, or were leaving Paris, and yet we still lingered on in our pretty apartment of the Avenue Gabriel.

One morning, suddenly looking up from my embroidery, I was struck with the pallor of Evelyn's countenance, and the look of weariness she wore. A book was lying open on a table near ; but she did not read. Silently she dreamed, her head resting on her hand.

"Dear Evelyn," I said, while she started as one aroused from sleep; "shall we not soon go to the country ? You look far from well—and Ella would cull fresh roses at the sea, or at Baden."

"Ella is very well," she answered listlessly, "and attends her classes daily. I, too, am well enough," and she heaved a sigh so heartsore it was almost a sob.

"Indeed, dearest, you have been suffering for three weeks—ever since the last ball at the Tuilleries, when you looked like a sunset cloud, as Mr. D'Arcy said." She gave a short, quick start, "all in golden colored tulle and hazy blonde. I never saw you look more lovely."

"Not enough," returned Evelyn gloomily, "would I were a thousand times more beautiful. Even then," she whispered, as if to herself, "I should not match with the matchless."

"Is it possible? and are you serious?" I said, painfully alive to her emotion; "is your happiness so entirely involved in——"

"In *him.* Yes, my kind — my too forbearing friend. Evelyn, the once idolized, petted, spoiled— the capricious, the heartless coquette—the once proud beauty—loves for the first time, with that love which is her doom. His presence is my light and life; his absence my soul's despair. And yet, Mary, not one word of love has he ever spoken; and since that ball he has never been here—never written—he so exact, so chivalrous in his politeness. Oh, Mary, why—why this so sudden change?"

She fixed her sad eyes, round which were two dark circles—sign of many a sleepless night—imploringly on my face.

" I will find out for you," I said; "you shall at
least be spared the pangs of suspense."

"Ah, me!" she murmured, " men little know the
hours of patient watching and waiting we poor women suffer. 'Tis not to be wondered at we make
the best Christians—'*the patience of hope.*' I understand it now."

I took a *coupé*, and in less than an hour I had returned, for D'Arcy resided in the Rue Castiglione.

Evelyn, still seated where I had left her, sprang
to her feet, almost shrieking as she saw my solemn
countenance, " Bad news! Oh, tell me the worst!"

" Mr. D'Arcy," I said, " is ill."

" Not dead!—not dead! Oh, speak!"

" No; but seriously ill."

" I will go to him, instantly."

" Stay, Evelyn," I said, with authority, " he is unworthy of your love."

She looked at me in blank astonishment.

"The fever he has, he caught in the low neigh-
borhoods, and among the disreputable company
he frequents."

She laughed hysterically.

" What!" she said, " the noble D'Arcy—the refined, the spiritual. Never, by my hopes of Heaven.
Go, Mary, would you have me hate you? Look

you, he is true and pure as the blessed sunlight.—
Unhand me, I say; let me fly to him."

" Oh! Evelyn, pause, I implore you. What will
the world say ?"

" What it likes. Ah! is it *my* Mary who would
dissuade me from tending a fellow-creature in sickness—a stranger in a strange land ? No; she will
rather assist me, and when exhausted nature re-
quires that the ' sister of mercy ' should take food
and rest, *my* Mary will then relieve her at her post."

Evelyn passed her arm caressingly around me.
How could I find it in my heart to refuse her? and
so our compact was sealed with a kiss.

It was time the sick man should have a tender
and loving nurse; he was suffering from a low, nervous fever, with typhoid symptoms superadded.—
Three physicians were in constant attendance. All
light in the chamber was strictly forbidden, and the
least noise caused the patient to start as at the fir-
ing of a park of artillery. Evelyn's first act was to
dismiss the coarse, fat nurse, who sat dozing and occasionally snoring in a comfortable easy-chair.—
Taking the authority of a sister upon her, she paid
the woman, and stated her firm intention of remaining the sole attendant at the bedside of her brother.
Then gently and softly she moved about, robed in a
peignoir of delicate white muslin, putting all in or-

der. The sick man—half delirious—seemed to feel there was some change, for he murmured tenderly, "what angel is here?" Evelyn gently laid her cool hand on the fevered brow, but spoke not, for to do so was forbidden. The touch soothed and quieted the sufferer, and the physicians, when they came, found a slight change for the better. For six days and nights did Evelyn and myself watch alternately by the bedside of poor D'Arcy, who in his moments of wandering, seemed earnestly engaged in conversation with a spirit he named as Lilian, his affianced bride. As if in reply, he would say:

"I will obey you implicitly. Lilian, my sweet sister, bride no longer, since you so will it. I have now another guardian angel near. Say you so? and you warn me not to pass by my destiny. You caution me against such blindness, and you leave me."

Much more was said, but so incoherent we could not gather the sense—and then, fatigued, the patient would dose off into the restless, unrefreshing sleep of fever. At length we could no longer deceive ourselves; the poor sufferer grew weaker and weaker, till at last the doctors unanimously shook their learned heads, and augured the worst. The principal physician, taking me apart, said,

"My dear lady, break it gently to the poor sister—for in twelve hours her brother will be no more."

Evelyn, pale as marble, and almost as cold and motionless, waved me off. She had heard too well the ominous whisper. For twelve long hours, her arm tenderly sustained the head of the dying man, the other hand ceaselessly engaged in the last painful offices of affection. Utterly forgetful of self— even of her overwhelming sorrow—her one thought was how she could best soften the parting agony. Every moment she listened for the almost imperceptible breathing, each instant feeling for the beating of the heart. But the pulse waxed fainter and fainter, the death-rattle came to the throat—a long, long sigh—another, and another—then the heart ceased to beat, and all was over.

The doctors ascertained the fact of the decease, and were too glad to leave the house of mourning. Evelyn, tearless, desolate, despairing, sank on her knees beside the couch—*she believed in prayers for the dead.* I knelt beside her, and our united supplications ascended to the throne of the Most High. At length I arose, and would have led the afflicted one away. She resisted. "I will not leave him," she said. Finding it useless endeavoring to change her resolve, I went home, and returned later, determined not to give up the point. Reluctantly the mourner consented to take some repose. She arose from her knees; then suddenly, and as one frantic, she flung herself upon the lifeless corpse.

"I will not leave thee, Philip—mine in death, if not in life."

She clung to the helpless clay, her warm, fresh mouth pressing the ice-cold lips, her pure breath entering the paralyzed lungs. The passionate heart, full of the magnetism of life, beating against that stone-cold breast—now, alas! still for ever.

"Philip," she cried again and again, straining the dear form closer and yet closer in her fond embrace, "come back to your Evelyn," when, O wondrous to relate! the spirit just about to take wing, and emerge from the dark terrors of the "valley of the shadow of death," or intermediate state, into life and immortality, paused,—wavered—looked back lovingly, and returned to the body. A Divine influx descending through that tender woman's bosom, established a human sympathy once more with the apparently lifeless frame, and D'Arcy again breathed the breath of life.

CHAPTER XXI.

E L L A .

EVELYN had saved Philip D'Arcy's life, but almost at the cost of her own. The reaction from intense despair to the excess of joy, was too much for her, and to a deathlike swoon succeeded the frantic ravings of delirium. The fever of her beloved had fastened its cruel fangs in her very vitals. During weeks and weeks of suffering, I scarcely left the bedside of my poor friend—for ever and for ever did she utter the name of Philip, her true mate, her celestial bridegroom, her first, last, her only love. Unwilling that other ears should discover the secret of her heart, I permitted none to approach, cautiously concealing from Ella the dangerous nature of the malady, lest the dear girl should insist on sharing my anxious watch, and thus be made aware of her mother's weakness—a weakness which, while pitying, I deeply deplored. Poor D'Arcy too, I remembered, must not be left

8*

alone with strangers. At my desire, therefore, Ella, accompanied by an elderly female attendant, supplied her mother's place in the sick room of him who still required the utmost attention and solicitude.

Many days elapsed ere the patient was pronounced out of danger, and permitted to speak.

"Sir, I am both surprised and happy to be able to announce your convalescence; and it is to the devoted attention of this young girl," designating Ella, "that, under divine Providence, you owe your life." So spake the man of science, not aware of the whole truth, as we know it, and he spake as he thought. The sick man turned a grateful look on his young nurse, gently raising the hand she had placed in his to his pallid lips.

Many a time, as he daily grew stronger, would D'Arcy desire to ask after Evelyn; and yet, simple as was the question, it appeared as if his tongue refused to frame it. "Strange that she never inquires—never comes," he mused. "Were not Ella so calm, I should say her mother, too, must be ill." At length, he determined to solve his doubts— "Your dear mother, my child, and Miss Mildmay— tell me of them ?"

"Poor mama," replied the young girl, "is not very well."

"Nothing serious, I trust."

"Oh! no. She caught cold, I believe, the last time she was out."

D'Arcy sighed—in his heart he maligned poor Evelyn as a true woman of the world, a fashionable coquette, heartless as she was beautiful; and thinking thus, he unconsciously watched the graceful, half-childish form of Ella, as she noiselessly stole about the room, or bent over her tapestry frame, till at length he grew to listen eagerly for her coming and regret her parting step. Sweetly would the tones of her silvery voice fall on his ear, as, reclining on a couch propped up by cushions, he listened while she read to him extracts from Byron, Wordsworth, Tennyson, or some noble bard of his own fair land. At such times he would name her, half in jest, "Elaine, the lily maid," who died of love for the brave Sir Launcelot.

One afternoon, as the invalid drew fresh life from the warm beams of the mid-day sun, his young companion, seated on a low stool at his feet, her fairy fingers busily engaged with her tapestry, D'Arcy said—"Sweet Elaine! shall we read, or shall we have a little quiet talk together?"

With a sweet smile, she answered, still diligently plying her needle: "We will converse to-day—for

I must finish this cushion for mama by the time she is quite well."

But D'Arcy appeared embarrassed; and, after a pause of some minutes' duration, he probably said just the thing he had never intended to utter :

"My child, could you love ?"

Wonderingly, Ella raised her soft blue eyes, and fixed them on the face of the speaker—" Why, certainly," she said; "I dearly, dearly love my mother."

" And none other ?"

"Oh! yes, indeed—Mary—our kind, good Mary, for example. You, too, of course," blushing slightly—" you are now another dear friend."

" But, Ella, listen. Could you, for instance, love as—as—Elaine loved Launcelot ?"

She paused. " I have never thought of that—at any rate, if he had not loved me, I should never have been so silly as to care for him."

" No—but supposing he had loved you ?"

" Well, in that case, perhaps I might; but, oh! Mr. D'Arcy, never, even then, nearly so much as I love my own dear mother. Ah! you do not know how I love her," and the tears started to the dear child's clear eyes; " but," she hesitated, "I *do* wish to say something to you—you must never, *never* mention it, though. Perhaps it is foolish to tell you—but, I should so like my mother to marry."

It now was D'Arcy's turn to feel his cheek all flame. "It is, doubtless," he forced himself to reply, "by your mother's own desire that she remains single."

"I do not know," mused Ella—"she was very nearly married once; but *it* (I mean the marriage) was postponed, in consequence of her not being willing to change her religion. I, however, know she loved the ——, but I will not name him."

D'Arcy was now pale as death. "Perhaps," said he, "all may at present be at an end."

"Oh! no, indeed," exclaimed Ella, eagerly; "they still correspond, I know—and he is *so* handsome, *so* good, *so* fond of her—she would be very, *very* happy—*do*, Mr. D'Arcy, persuade mama to become a Catholic!"

He seemed lost in thought. "Sweet Elaine," at length he said, "rest assured, that, to further your mother's welfare and your own, I would gladly sacrifice my life. I will take an early occasion of conversing with her on this subject."

Meanwhile, my poor invalid lay turning and tossing on her fevered couch, and ever and forever would she thus make moan: "Philip, my own true mate — Philip, bridegroom of my soul — why so

cruel?" Then, in her wild delirium, would she
sing snatches of melody, and her voice was strong,
clear, and of unearthly sweetness. Often would she
repeat those exquisite lines of Shelly :

"The nightingale's complaint, it dies upon her heart,
    As I must on thine, beloved as thou art—
    A spirit hath led me to thee, love."

"Yes, Lilian—thy loved Lilian, hath given thee
to Evelyn—Reginald, too, looks upon me with tender and forgiving eyes. See! they descend together to bless our union—they bear a wreath of
orange blossoms and myrtle—they place it on my
burning brow—it is cool—cool—delicious! Oh!
what fragrance! It soothes my brain—it recalls
my senses—the dews of Paradise fall like a shower
of pearls over my tangled hair. Ah! see—they
place a white moss rose on my bosom—it stills the
throbbings of my heart—it deadens the pain!
Thanks, blessed, loving angels! Pray for poor
Evelyn. She is saved!"

As she uttered these words an exquisite perfume
filled the sick chamber, and I saw, as it were, a
halo of white light around the head of the poor sufferer, and fancied I beheld a hand, white as alabas-
ter, holding a rose to her breast. A moment, and
the light faded, or rather, gave place to the sickly

rays of the early dawn, as they penetrated the closed blinds and shone on the pale form of the patient. Was this a vision or a mere disorder of the fancy? I know not; but I do know that from that moment the fever left her; that she slept profoundly for twelve consecutive hours; and on awakening was declared convalescent.

CHAPTER XXII.

IT was the sixteenth of August; the heat had been intense, but toward evening a cool air stirred the leaves of the trees, and entered the open window of the pretty boudoir in the Avenue Gabriel. That day our beloved invalid·quitted her room for the first time. Languidly reclining on an elegant couch of pale green silk, her sweet face half buried in the rich lace which ornamented the downy cushions, she enjoyed the voluptuous sensations incident to the convalescent state. Ella had decked the apartment with flowers, to *fête* the recovery of her dear mother, and a silver tea-service, standing on a small table near, plentifully supplied with cakes and fruit, added greatly to the home comfort of the scene.

Evelyn's illness, if it had somewhat detracted

from the brilliancy of her beauty, had replaced it with an air of delicacy and refinement, which, perhaps, suited still better the classic outline of her features. Her complexion, transparent as porcelain, was now colorless, if we except a bright spot on either cheek—the result of emotion rather than of returning health. Her soft, hazel eyes seemed humid with a tender languor which gave to them a remarkable charm. The warm pulses of renewed life and hope seemed to pervade each nerve and fibre of her being. I could scarcely keep my eyes from looking at her, while Ella, echoing my thoughts, exclaimed:

"Dearest mama, how very beautiful you look this evening!"

The mother pensively smiled, passed her hand through her daughter's hair, and then was again lost in thought.

But let us now permit her to speak for herself.

MORE LEAVES.

August 16th.—It is nearly three whole months since I have seen him, and oh! what events since then. Both have been sick nigh unto death; both have received revelations from the angel world, and I shall see him this day, and he said to Ella he would speak with me alone. Ah! the cruel moments lengthen themselves into hours to retard his coming. And if, after all, he should fail. But that is not possible, has he not given his word!

17*th*.—I have made a violent effort to collect my scattered senses, for I would fain write the occurrences of *that* night. Though the day appeared as if it would never end, yet, as evening approached, I almost dreaded to meet him. The thought that I had dared to clasp him, living, in my arms—that unasked, unsought, my lips had been pressed to his, made me timid as a young girl. This remembrance, even now, dyes my cheek with crimson. Oh! were he then conscious of all, how could I ever, ever, again lift my eyes to his; how could I ever support his glance of withering scorn. As these reflections passed through my brain, I half arose. "I will retire to my room," I thought, "and leave Mary and Ella to receive him." Just then there was a ring, and a well-known step was heard in the antecham-ber. Philip D'Arcy entered, and in the delirious joy of his presence, I forgot all but that he was here once more—restored to life, to health, to hope, to love. He appeared surprised to find me still an invalid, for as he took my hand and pressed it with that soft, thrilling pressure which may mean friend-

ship, or so much more, he murmured words of
sorrow and sympathy, though I scarcely caught
their meaning. Then seating himself, as Mary
served the tea, he addressed some polite and commonplace observations to her and Ella. I could
now satisfy the hunger of my soul by dwelling on
that noble countenance, the light of which had so
long been hidden from my weary eyes.

After long silence, I said suddenly,

"Pray, Mr. D'Arcy, tell me how did you manage to catch that fever?"

The formality of this address sounded strangely
even to my own ears, and almost as if another had
spoken.

Philip smiled his old smile, and replied that he
would prefer this should remain a secret. Perceiving a somewhat mocking expression on Mary's lips,
I exclaimed with petulance,

"But I insist on your telling me—I *will* know."

Turning upon me a calm and penetrating, though
rather surprised look, he said quietly,

"I have the gift of healing by mesmeric passes ;
over fatigued by too close attendance on a patient
suffering from a virulent attack of morbid typhus,
I saved him, but succumbed to the malady myself."

I cast a triumphant glance at Mary. It was with
difficulty I could resist the impulse I felt to throw

myself at his feet, almost in adoration. Mary then
happily observed, in her usual calm and philosophic
style, that " magnetism appeared to be the grand
motive power of organic nature."

"Say rather," replied D'Arcy, " of the entire
visible universe. Do we not know that the poles
of the earth are magnetic? Is there not electro-
magnetism in the sun's beams? And in fact I have
very little doubt that the power named gravita-
tion by Newton, is neither more nor less than magnetic attraction."

"That," replied Mary, " is both a philosophic
and a beautiful idea."

" I think," rejoined he, " it at least bears the
impress of truth, and as science progresses, who
knows whether it will not be ascertained that similar internal laws govern these apparently distinct
forces? All true science tends towards unity, as
all religions point to the ONE TRUE GOD."

So passed the time, till tea being over, Mary with
Ella proposed taking a stroll—the latter laughingly
saying that the two invalids might amuse each other
by expatiating on the delights of panada, *tisane*,
and chicken broth.

In the sweet hour of twilight, alone once
more with *him*, and awaiting, as it were, the
fiat of my destiny, is it wonderful that pale with
emotion I lay almost as one inanimate?

"I fear"—and the tones of his voice were low and tender as he bent over me—"I fear me much you still suffer."

"I have been ill, very ill," I murmured, scarcely daring to trust my voice.

"Can you listen," he almost whispered, "if I speak to you on a subject important to me, interesting to you—to both——"

I signed assent, for I was powerless now to articulate one word.

"During my illness," he proceeded, "I was in constant communication with the spirit of my Lilian. Much advice she gave, and much she cautioned as to my future; finally, she informed me that it was not her destiny to become my bride through eternity, but that there was one then near who would save my life—one whose tender bosom would ever pulsate in unison with my own, whose character of mind and heart was, from contrast, fitted alone to complete mine—'but,' she added, solemnly, 'make not shipwreck of your happiness. *Pass not by your fate.*'"

He paused. I could make no reply. My blood was coursing rapidly and tumultuously through every vein and artery. My voice, passion-choked, could only express itself in sighs. My soul seemed bathed in an ocean of hitherto unknown delights. I

scarcely dared breathe, lest I should lose a word,
a tone. A few moments more of suspense would
have killed me. Would that it had been so!

Soft as the murmur of a summer brook, thrilling
as the song of birds, tender as the cooing of the
wood-pigeon, did that loved voice again steal upon
my ear. "At one time," it said, "methought I was
dying. I lost all physical sensation. My heart felt
like a stone in the midst of my body. My breathing seemed to be carried on through the spiritual
lungs alone—when, suddenly, as if from afar, I
heard, as it were, a faint cry—a cry of distress:
'Philip, mine own, do not die,' it said, 'Return—
oh! return.' (I covered my burning face with my
hands, as he continued.)

"At this time I felt on my lips a warm breath—a
human heart appeared to touch my own—then all
was dark, dark. On opening my eyes, I beheld, as
an angel of light, standing at my bedside, your
sweet child Ella."

As if one had taken a sledge-hammer, and struck
with violence a blow on the very centre of my
heart—such was the shock I experienced. Stunned,
unconscious, I heard no more. Had it not been
thus mercifully arranged, I had not stifled a burst
of passionate anguish. When I in some measure recovered my senses a mortal despair seized upon me.

The shades of evening had now closed in, my soul too was all gloom. Still those soft accents fell on my ear, till at length I distinguished the words, " Have I then your consent?" In vain would I have replied, but my throat was parched—my tongue paralyzed. I could only bend my head in token of assent. " On one other subject would I also for a moment speak," and then the beloved voice trembled and faltered, " Pardon me, but your happiness is dear—dearer to me than my own. I understand," —he hesitated, and then spoke rapidly, as though he would be rid of an ungrateful task, " I hear, there is one who adores you—one who has haply not loved in vain—one, in fine, who even now stands toward you in the light of an affianced husband. May I express the hope that this union will no longer be delayed, and that bliss such as rarely falls to mortal lot may be yours, and his for your sweet sake?" Philip raised my hand to his lips. " Good God?" he cried, " you are ill—your hand is cold and clammy as in death."

I tried to smile. Happily the darkness covered the ghastly and futile attempt. By a supreme effort I rose to my feet.

" I am well. I thank you," I gasped, " for—for your good wishes. I shall"—and I pressed both hands on my heart to still its wild beatings, now and forever, if I could—"I shall marry soon—very soon."

Staggering to the door, I met Mary and Ella.—Motioning the latter toward the boudoir, and clinging almost fainting to Mary, who caught me in her arms, I was half-led, half-carried to my bed-chamber —where, left alone with my grief, my despair, my lost love, my wounded woman's pride—worn out by that "hope deceived which maketh the heart sick," exhausted nature could no more, and sleep at length in pity steeped my weary soul in forgetfulness.

CHAPTER XXIII.

LOVED IN VAIN.

Is there one among us who has not, at some period of his life, experienced the dull pain which, on the morrow of a great grief, ever returns to us with the first dawn of consciousness? Have we not hated the very light of another day? Have not all familiar objects lost their charm for us? How sensitively, too, have we shrunk from contact with the domestics—aye, even from the loved faces of the home circle! Alone would we entertain our sorrow. We are in love with her, and from her we will not be parted. This is the very luxury of grief. Joy may be a social passion; but surely the converse is true of profound misery.

Our unhappy heroine dared not thus indulge her sorrow—she must up and be doing. The poisoned arrow which had pierced her bosom must there remain, an agonized but concealed torture. Ah! me—those pangs for which the world would have no pity, and

9

which, therefore, we must hide under the semblance of smiles, are ever the most poignant.

Like lawful love, legitimate grief may be deep; but neither are of that stormy nature which shakes the soul to its foundation, and blights the whole existence. So Evelyn arose, mechanically, and suffered her maid to attire her; then, causing the blinds to be closed, the better to conceal her haggard countenance, she bade the attendant leave the room.

To the question—"Will madame take breakfast now?" her mistress replied, that she merely required a cup of tea; and added, that, having important letters to write, she must not for the present be disturbed. Then flinging herself into a chair, and covering her aching eyes with her hand, she endeavored to collect her thoughts. Just then, she felt a soft warm touch—when, starting, she turned and perceived her faithful dog, the gift of di Balzano. He had placed his paw in her hand, and he looked into her face with a fond, wistful glance, which seemed to say, "Dear mistress, you are sick or sad; but your poor dog loves you, and will never forsake you." And Evelyn comprehended, and she flung her arm about the shaggy neck of her favorite, and the large scalding drops fell on his honest head. "Poor Dashey," she said—"poor fellow!"—and tears,

too, almost human, stood in the eyes of the loving
animal. Nay, mock not, gentle reader—for, as the
author has observed, so she writes. She once had a
dog whom she has seen weep more than once; and
when the poor fond creature died, she mourned for
her (for she was of the softer sex) as for a friend.

And Evelyn went to her writing-table—her resolve was taken. "Good, kind Balzano," she said;
"how he loved me—unworthy as I am! I will no
longer delay writing to him;" and she penned the
letter we here transcribe:

A Sua Excellenza, il Duca di Balzano,
Palazzo Balzano, Naples, August —, 18—.

DEAR FRIEND,—Pardon my prolonged silence,
and apparent neglect. I have been ill—danger-
ously ill—for many weeks. Before that, I had
come to no decision on the subject of your last letter. I cannot be a Catholic; but, if you can procure a dispense from the Pope, I will now be your
wife. Can you forgive my caprice! At last, I
understand how cruelly you must have suffered
through me. Henceforth, it will be the sole aim of
my life to compensate for past folly, by future devotion to your happiness. Write soon, and say when
we may expect you here. Ella you will find grown
out of all knowledge. You were ever a favorite

'with her. I cannot write more. I am still very
weak—but, as ever,

Your affectionate friend,

EVELYN.

The letter was just concluded, when a gentle tap
at the door caused the writer's heart to give one
bound, and then almost to cease beating. Evelyn
withdrew the bolt—for she must speak with Ella.
The young girl threw herself on her mother's neck;
but that mother's kiss was cold, for the first time—
and, as she felt the soft contact of her child's pure
lips, almost a shudder passed through her frame.
Ah! wherefore did the shadow of *that man* come
between those two! And Ella knelt at her mother's
feet, an unconscious rival; and as the latter, faint
and sick at heart, leaned back in her *fauteuil*, she
held the poor burning hand in her cool fresh palm,
and poured out before her mother all the thoughts
and feelings of her innocent, loving heart. She
told how D'Arcy loved her, how kind he was,
how clever—far too wise and clever for her, how
could he think of such a child? True, Lilian had
told him, or it could never have been; but her
dear mother must teach her to become wise, worthy of him, that he may not think her foolish—
"But oh! my own, own mama, I never, never

will marry and leave you all alone. I told Mr.
D'Arcy so. Never till you are a duchess, you
know," kissing her hand, "for though I like him
very much, I never shall love him like my own
sweet mother; how could I!"

Alas! poor Evelyn; bitterly did thy heart reproach thee that thou couldst not feel as the tender
maiden at thy feet—that thy now guilty love still
glowed in thy tortured heart, as in a furnace, to the
exclusion of each gentle and more holy sentiment.
Unhappy mother! she could scarce support the presence of her child now.

"Dear girl," she said, with an effort, "be happy. I have written to accept M. di Balzano."—
Ella made a movement of delight. "Bless you,
darling, now leave me. Take that letter and see
that it is sent. I would be alone, my head aches
terribly." A true woman's excuse, but in our heroine's case not a fictitious one.

Once more left to her own sad thoughts, Evelyn
endeavored to realize her painful position. It was
necessary to meet D'Arcy; to show him that she
consented, nay, that she was even happy, in the
idea of his union with another, and that other her
own daughter. "Alas!" she repeated to herself,

"To love thee dumbly, nor by look or word
  To break the silence set upon my soul,
  To crush the voice that struggles to be heard,
  To gaze unmoved on the forbidden goal.

"To sit and look into thine eyes, and yearn
  To tell thee all my closely hoarded thought,
  And still to know that I must calmly learn
  To meet thy gaze, and yet to utter naught

"To know there is no hope; hourly to feel
  That Destiny forbids a word, a breath;
  This bitter fate is mine, until the seal
  Is broken, by the welcome hand of death."

And she accepted her fate, and she made the heroic resolve — cost what it might, she would see D'Arcy this evening, if but for five minutes. She would school her eyes to gaze calmly on those still beloved features. She would force herself to support the sight of those lover-like attentions which were not, which never could be for her. She would even be happy in the mutual happiness of those two dear ones. Did she, perchance, miscalculate her strength? For the present, at least, that trial was spared her. Just about the hour D'Arcy's visit was expected, a telegraphic despatch arrived from Havre. It was handed to me by Evelyn to open and read. It ran thus:

" Pressing public business recalls me to America.
I sail to-night. Will write from Cowes.

"Philip D'Arcy."

A sigh of inexpressible relief burst from Evelyn's
overcharged bosom, as she murmured involuntarily,
"Thank God." Last evening, at the same hour
had an event so unexpected occurred, how different
would have been her feelings! Truly "we know
not what a day may bring forth."

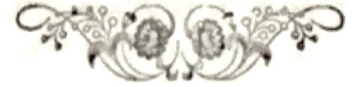

CHAPTER XXIV.

Two days and the promised letter arrived, the very superscription and seal proclaiming it the production of no ordinary writer. Opening the missive you at once remark the clear, decided, manly characters. No dashes, (impotent attempts of weakness to convey the idea of force), deface the spotless page; the style terse, and at the same time elegant, reveals the scholar and the gentleman. The signature, at once bold and distinct, has the characteristic finish, rather than flourish, which at once individualizes the writer. Truly there is more in an autograph than meets the eye of the casual observer. Give me a letter and I will undertake to designate the salient points in the character and disposition of its author. The epistle in question was addressed to Evelyn, and simply stated that public affairs having assumed a very serious aspect, he (D'Arcy), had received a mandate from an official personage, requesting his immediate presence at Washington, and offering him a responsible post under government. That in view of the present sad political difficulties which threatened his beloved country, he thought it his duty to tender his poor services to the nation. Though his affections, he added, were dear —most dear to him—still he felt that honor and duty must take precedence even of love. In conclusion he expressed the hope of a speedy return to Europe, but added that as his sweet Ella's extreme youth rendered an immediate marriage unadvisable, he would wait with patience, convinced that every additional moment passed with her dear and valued mother, would be fraught with inestimable advantage to his young bride. Leaving her, therefore, to Evelyn, as a sacred charge, he invoked on the beloved heads of both a farewell blessing.

Such was D'Arcy's first letter. Single hearted, true and noble, he framed no polite excuses for apparent neglect in not having called to bid them a personal adieu. He knew they would understand him, and he was right. It now appeared to me that there was a marked change in Evelyn. All her passionate love for D'Arcy seemed to have merged into a fond desire to educate Ella for him. She accepted the holy task he had confided to her, and made a firm resolve to devote her faculties wholly

9*

to the furtherance of his wishes. Thus, no longer
living as before utterly in the self-hood, but rather
seeking the good of others, she could not fail to
bring a blessing on herself.

We passed the remainder of the summer at Passy,
near Paris, where Rossini has a beautiful villa, and
where, others of our friends were also residing. Ex-
pecting shortly the arrival of Balzano, we had
thought it inexpedient to journey further. But
weeks were added to days, and months to weeks,
and yet no letter came " He will doubtless come
without writing," we said, and so saying, daily
looked we for his advent. Our frequent talk now
was of beloved Italy, and of the happy days we had
passed beneath the placid azure of its heavens.

"Ah! me," sighed my friend, "how rarely do
we value the present till it has faded into the past!
We spend our lives in wild hopes of the future—in
sad regrets for bygone days. Folly—to the present
with its pleasures and pains may we alone lay claim as
our own. Do you remember, Mary, the fairy-like *fête*
given by the Conte de Syracuse, in that exquisitely
lovely mountain glade at Castellamare, so shadowy
with graceful trees, through whose branches here
and there, a bright glint of sunshine gilded the rocks,
dancing over the feathery fern, and causing the rivulet
to sparkle with a clearer crystal? how sapphire blue

lay the Mediterranean, viewed through the interstices of the varied foliage. It was truly a scene of enchantment, and reminded me of those days chronicled by Boccaccio when six gallant cavaliers with their noble dames retired together to the fair gardens of *Sans Souci* that they might avoid the in fection of the pestilence then desolating the doomed city of Florence."

"Yes," said I, "and how picturesque the table prepared as it were, by the genii of the forest; how brilliant the dresses of the ladies, and though last, not least, how cool and refreshing the well iced champagne! And, after the collation, how charmingly wild our dance on the greensward to the stirring music of the invisible orchestra deeply hidden in the woods."

"And the Prince, too, how wickedly and maliciously he insisted on the stout old Baroness de R—— being his partner in the polka, till she looked actually purple, so that we feared every minute her desire to oblige H. R. H. would cause her to faint with fatigue. Oh! Mary, those were merry days! The silver moon arose to look upon our sport, and the fire-flies came and danced with us."

"And you remember the pretty compliment the Prince paid you, Evelyn, about the pearls? You had your hair braided, and bonnet trimmed with these ornaments—bracelets and necklace to match. His Royal Highness said ' Pearls in the hair, on the neck, and the rounded white arms, but the finest pearls of all are within the rosy lips.' "

"Ah! Mary, remind me not of my days of vanity and folly. Have I not sufficiently suffered for my poor triumphs? Had I been less handsome I might have been a better and a happier woman."

" You may yet be both, dearest, it is not too late."

Thus time passed, and we returned to Paris, no reply having as yet arrived from Naples, so we began to think that, (as is frequently the case there), Evelyn's letter might have miscarried. She was just preparing to write again, when one morning Ella entered, frantic with delight.

" A letter! a letter!" she exclaimed, " from dear Italy. What will mama give for it? a kiss—no, two, at least three—there," and Evelyn took it, and broke the seal. It was in di Balzano's fine Italian hand, and as follows:

Naples, Nov. —, 18—.

MY DEAR MRS. TRAVERS: I feel much distressed and mortified in that I fear you must have considered me ungrateful, and wanting in politeness; but you will, I trust, now pardon the silence I have been compelled to observe towards you. It is time I should inform you that I am already married. Such, however, being the case, remember it is yourself who have constrained me to this step, by your in- decision. But we will no longer speak of the past. May I hope that being made aware of my marriage will not prevent your still preserving for me that same friendship you have ever accorded to one who will never cease most deeply to appreciate it. For my part, I should be truly delighted once more to meet you, because I still feel for you a profound affection; having once loved you intensely and passionately. I am thankful that your health is re- established. Saluting you a thousand times, I am as ever your true friend,

GIOVANNI, DUCA DI BALZANO.

"See, Mary," said poor Evelyn, handing me the letter with a melancholy smile, "it is my sad doom to lose all I love, all that have loved me!"

We heard later that Balzano's marriage had originated first, as is the custom in Italy, in the wishes of the respective families of the young peo- ple, the duke being averse to the connexion. Bal- zano was thus necessarily much thrown into the society of the young lady, who became deeply at- tached to him—so much so, that perceiving his in- difference she took it so seriously to heart that consumption threatened. Balzano, ever compassionate and unselfish, pitied the girl, and not having for months had any tidings of his former betrothed, consented at last to the wishes of his friends, backed by the advice of the priests. A marriage was arranged; singularly enough, it was not till his return from church, on the morning of the wedding, that Evelyn's letter of acceptance was placed in his hands—thus may the three months' silence, on his part, he accounted for.

Meanwhile, D'Arcy's letters came almost every mail; they were partly to Evelyn, partly to Ella; and were answered conjointly by both. Ella would have deferred the marriage indefinitely, in consequence of the bad news from Naples; but her mother would not suffer the subject even to be alluded to: "My child," she said, "let us leave the future to Providence, patiently awaiting the accomplishment of our destiny."

CHAPTER XXV.

THE BARONET.

AMONG the crowd of English sojourning in Paris this winter, there was an old acquaintance of ours —a certain Sir Percy Montgomery, Bart., late M. P. for ——shire. Some six years ago, when in London, Sir Percy had visited Evelyn, and we had dined occasionally at his house in Grosvenor Street. Indeed, the Baronet had been at that time a warm though unsuccessful admirer of our heroine. Sir Percy was, in appearance, a perfect "John Bull"—that is to say, he possessed a countenance rubicund and somewhat flat, with no very marked features—figure stout—burly—broad-shouldered— thick set, you perceived at a glance that the animal nature preponderated in the man; nevertheless, the square and rather massive forehead displayed intellect, and the fine teeth, seen to advantage in a pleasant jovial smile of not unfrequent occurrence, rendered the personal appearance of our friend, if

somewhat coarse, not altogether unpleasing. Let
not my readers, however, imagine that the
"John-Bull" type is the true type of our countrymen. They will, on referring to a former chapter
of this work, find the portrait of an accomplished
English gentleman, in our delineation of the young
and aristocratic Melville. We have there depicted
elegance, manliness and chivalry, in combination
with the splendid physical development, only to be
seen in perfection in the Anglo-Saxon race. But, to
return. Sir Percy was by no means wanting in
brains. He had made some sensation in Parlia-
ment; and, having had the tact to speak on the
popular side of each question, his fluency was
greatly appreciated, and he had thus acquired a
higher reputation than his (not first rate) talents
perhaps merited. So the Times wondered when he
resigned his seat; and the Herald and other Tory
papers were open in their rather uncharitable sur-
mises, as to the motives for so sudden and untimely
a retreat in the late M. P.

Sir Percy, having discovered our address at Ga-
lignani's, lost no time in paying his respects to Evelyn, and continued his visits from time to time.
Evelyn soon named him my adorer, and said it would
not be such a bad match; the baronet was of a good
family, and reputed rich, though, as some asserted,

rich in debts alone. He had, at least, talent, and if
I did not object to his lack of personal beauty, and
his fifty years, she added, I might do worse than become Lady Montgomery. Ever occupied with receiving and replying to D'Arcy's frequent letters,
or in reading, talking and practising with Ella, my
friend paid but slight attention to a former admirer
—for whom she had never felt even a passing gleam
of sympathy—until one day she received from him
a rather melancholy letter; making her in some sort
a confidante, the writer threw out dark hints of
debts and difficulties which had exiled him from his
native land, and adverted mysteriously to envious
political rivals, who were endeavoring to work his
ruin, and who had, alas! succeeded in putting a
present stop to a career which would have otherwise shortly ended in the Cabinet. Much changed
for the better, since her acquaintance with Philip
D'Arcy, and somewhat hurt and humiliated by the
unexpected marriage of di Balzano, our heroine
opened her heart in pity for the baronet's misfor-
tunes; had not she, too, suffered from envious
tongues? had not slander been to her as "the worm
which never dieth?" Cruel, cruel world! thou art
indeed a hard master—offend against thy laws—
break thy one commandment "Thou shalt not be
found out" and thou art utterly without pity, even

to the exclusion of all repentance ;—cruel, cruel world! And so Evelyn took compassion on the injured man, and invited him oftener, and sympathized with his griefs, and was in every way kind to him. Thus did circumstances favor his suit.

So it came to pass that society at last coupled their names together, and Sir Percy himself, mistaking the sentiments of one who no longer had a heart to give, made our heroine an offer of his hand in a letter which appeared to me to allude to the lady's fortune rather than to herself. Evelyn answered that she would take time to consider the proposal, provided Sir Percy could assure her on his honor as a gentleman that there was no blemish attached to his name. This assurance, as may be imagined, the baronet readily gave. My dearest friend then spoke to me fully and confidentially ; frankly confessing that she no longer hoped for happiness on earth, she at the same time added, that she was anxious to marry, hoping that enshrined within the sacred precincts of a husband's home, and safely sheltered by his protection, she should have strength to crush forever from out her heart that now guilty passion which still tortured her.

" I could not," she continued, " again meet D'Arcy except as a wife—no. I too much fear my own weakness. I should sink to the earth with

shame, did he for one moment suspect the state
of my heart. Besides, I gave him my word I
would marry, and at any cost I will keep my prom
ise. Ella, too, dear child, is firmly resolved never
to wed till she sees her mother, as she imagines,
happy. Ah! Mary, does not this man's offer appear to you as it does to me, almost as a providen-
tial occurrence?"

"Had you not better at least wait Mr. D'Arcy's
next letter before you give a definite reply to Sir
Percy?"

"Yes, my friend, I will wait. You are right.
Dear Mary, my soul is bound up in the future happiness of Philip and that of my Ella, but like St.
Paul I may say, "I feel two laws warring within
me, and these are contrary, the one to the other, so
that when I would do good, evil is present with
me."

And the expected letter came, and it stated that
war having been declared between the North and
South, it was quite impossible for D'Arcy to leave
his post. Nor could he forsee when he dared hope
to return to Europe. Could not his beloved friends,
he suggested, all come over to New York next summer? He would place at their disposition *The Retreat*, a villa beautifully situated on the banks of
the Hudson, which it would afford him the greatest

pleasure if they would occupy as long as the weather should render such a sojourn agreeable. In conclusion, he reminded Evelyn, that being already
familiar with the continent of Europe, the difference
of scenery and the manner of living in the New
World, would greatly interest her, and that she
would find in this splendid country much to compensate her for the fatigues of the voyage. D'Arcy
had never in any letter alluded either directly or in-
directly to our heroine's projected marriage, nor had
he ever known the name of her probable husband,
the fact alone of her engagement having been com-
municated to him by the imprudence of Ella.

That same day Evelyn wrote an acceptance to
Sir Percy Montgomery.

And Ella—was she charmed with her mother's
present prospects? Truth compels us to declare she
was not; nor djd she ever cease expressing to me
her lively regret that her mama was so unwise as to
prefer the baronet to dear, good, handsome Balzano,
who was likewise of higher rank, and also of one
of the oldest families of mediæval Italy. But Ella had
not, as we know, been made aware of the chain of
circumstances which led to such a step on her mother's part; so she contented herself by adding, as a
last consolation, in the only Latin words she knew,
"*di gustibus non est disputandem.*" Since, then,

we cannot "account for tastes," still less may we understand the multiform caprices of beauty. This, however, I will say, and I appeal to the lovely of my own sex who have passed the age of thirty, to corroborate my assertion : Is there not some period in the life of each woman, when she would scarcely have thought any one worthy of herself? And is there not, likewise, another period, when, in her isolation, she might have been tempted to marry the first eligible person who asked her? I fear me such is too often the case.

I will here mention an incident which occurred à propos to this marriage : One evening, after dinner, Ella complaining of a headache, her mother, as was her wont, made over her a few mesmeric passes, in order to quiet the nerves. The young girl slept the magnetic sleep, as we perceived by the rigidity of the muscles, and other signs understood by the initiated. As Ella slept, I placed in her hand a letter, which had just chanced to arrive from Sir Percy. Instantly she became convulsed ; and, crushing the paper in her slender fingers, she flung it suddenly from her, exclaiming—

"I will not look at that man ; take him out of my sight—he has no heart—no honor."

The clairvoyante trembled violently, drawing her breath with difficulty. We did not dare force her to continue looking upon a disagreeable object; for, by such means, epileptic convulsions have been occasionally induced in an impressible subject, and sometimes even death has been known to supervene.

So Evelyn took her hand, as she now tranquilly slept, saying, "Then tell me, sweet one, shall I be happy?"

An angelic smile broke over the features of the lovely entranced, as she exclaimed, " You, dearest mother! Oh, yes—by your talents, your superior mind, your beautiful soul—not else," and she sighed.

Evelyn then awoke the young girl, who of course was aware of nothing that had passed during her mesmeric sleep; but her mother mused and wondered, and again I trembled for the future.

CHAPTER XXVI.

THREE MONTHS OF MARRIED LIFE.

It was in her second wifehood that Evelyn, Lady Montgomery, first set foot on the shores of the New World. Our voyage across the broad Atlantic had been devoid of incident, and untroubled by storm. An occasional squall, it is true, would banish us for a day to our heaving couches, where, prostrate and utterly helpless, we felt as if our head, detached from our shoulders, were rolling about the cabin, and the malignant sprites of ocean were recklessly and remorselessly sporting with it as with a foot-ball.

We entered the magnificent bay of New York, lighted by the glorious August moon with her myriads of attendant stars, which, seen through the pure ether of the western firmament, seemed multi plied to infinity. The constellations of the belted Orion, the greater and lesser Bear, and others, appeared strangely familiar; viewing them, we were fain to forget the thousands of miles which now

separated us from the land of our birth. But our
first step on terra firma quickly dispelled the illusion. The disagreeables of the Custom House at
an end, leaving our heavy baggage till the morrow,
with difficulty we climbed into the heavy, hearse-
like vehicle in waiting, which it seemed next to impossible to enter, and once in, equally vain and futile
to attempt the getting out. Tossed and tumbled
about on the roughest of pavements, our heads still
giddy from our recent sea-voyage, we arrived at
that gorgeous palace, yclept the Fifth Avenue Hotel. Happily, Mr. D'Arcy, (unable through press of
public business to meet us,) had kindly written to
secure rooms, which insured to our party the attention we should not otherwise have received.

Here let me observe that I entirely endorse all
that my talented countryman, Anthony Trollope,
has stated regarding the inhospitality of the enor-
mous American hotels, where weary and travel-
worn ladies are forced to await in the wretched reception parlors, the often long delayed advent of the
official charged to show them their rooms, while
gentlemen, still more unfortunate, must attend in
the office the favor for which they have humbly
made supplication to His Majesty the Book-keeper.
How different from the hearty welcome of " Mine
Host" and his worthy spouse, in the cheerful, old-

fashioned inns of England; how cheerily the land-
lord enters, and stirring the fire, makes his guests
feel instantly at home; while the good wife, were you
an old acquaintance, could not proffer for you with
greater kindness the best fare her house can afford.
The pretty chambermaid, too, candle in hand, shows
you to a clean, comfortable bedroom, leaving at the
same time, all the requisites for your toilet; and as
you discuss your cutlet or roast chicken, the waiter
tells you of all to be seen in the town and neighborhood. He closes the shutters and draws the curtains,
and your glass of sherry or old port, as may be,
has quite a home flavor, as you draw your easy-chair
cosily before the bright, glad fire, which itself sparkles and crackles its welcome.

I am not now describing the London or new railway
hotels, Heaven forbid! they are less comfortable, and
far more expensive than those in America; but I allude to the charming "hostelries" of the olden times,
some of which still exist, though "few and far between." Thanks, however, to the kind consideration
of Mr. D'Arcy, we were ushered at once to our
suite of elegantly furnished rooms, only too thankful to seek and find repose in the luxurious beds of
this splendid Hotel. On awakening, next morning,
my first impression of New-York was as if I saw
pictured before me, in giant proportions, one of the

toy towns with their many colored houses, interspersed with green trees, that used to come to me
in large oval deal boxes in the days of my youth.
Red brick, grey, brown, white, dark chocolate stone
—all of multiform size and shape, such is the description of the dwellings, in this metropolis of the
west, now decked in its mantle of summer foliage.

Our heroine had been wedded about three
months—was she blessed in her second union more
than in her first marriage?

My kind and gentle readers, she was not happy—
yet she was content. But had she ever before
indulged in any illusions, as regards Sir Percy, they
must have quickly faded. Even on returning
from the Church, his bride at his side, not one word
of affection did the newly made husband utter; of
himself alone he spoke—*his* position, *his* future; but
then, to be sure, he was turned of fifty, and as
Byron observes, rather than one husband at that
mature age,

>   "'Twere better to have *two*, at five-and-twenty."

This was the beginning of sorrows.

Immediately after the breakfast, the impatient
bridegroom, anxious, doubtless, to embrace the fair
lady he dared now call his own, knocked at the door

of her chamber, where, divested of her bridal costume, she was arraying herself in a becoming travelling toilette. When admitted, the grateful lover begged—now guess, dear ladies. I pray what —— Why for the loan of a few hundred francs to pay his bill at the hotel. Rather early, methinks, to usurp marital rights over his wife's purse. Poor Evelyn's next fit of disgust was on the morrow of her bridal, when, in an elegant morning robe of the freshest muslin, her hair braided under-the prettiest of caps, she with horror beheld Sir Percy enter the room, unwashed, uncombed, unbraced, and perfectly innocent of a clean shirt. Seating himself at the breakfast table, he commenced feeding, utterly unconscious of having committed an unpardonable crime against good manners. Unfortunate Evelyn! so refined, so fastidious, so exquisitely neat and clean in her personal habits, to be brought to this. "Oh! what a falling off was there!"

Sir Percy united in his own person those opposite defects which in others are usually compensated by corresponding virtues. He was at the same time a spendthrift, and the meanest of men. Hasty and imprudent, yet sly and cunning, with an appearance of frankness, he combined an utter disregard of truth. He seemed to lie for the pleasure of lying. His temper was alike quick, vindictive, and

revengeful, and his character comprised the opposite qualities of weakness and obstinacy. A general
lover of the female sex, he was utterly incapable of
individual attachment. It was clear that the baronet had married for money, but finding that his wife
contented herself simply with paying their mutual expenses, and refused to place her fortune in his power,
he actually began to dislike her and made no secret
of the feeling. One illustration I will give, and this
is but a solitary instance of the extraordinary line
of conduct pursued by Sir Percy towards her he had
so recently sworn to love, protect and cherish during
the term of their natural life.

Angered one night because Evelyn had left him a
small portion of his own travelling expenses to pay,
he rang up the servants of the hotel at midnight, and
though we were to start on the following morning at
break of day, he ordered his luggage to be transport-
ed and his bed made in a room at the most distant end
of the corridor, thus making himself and his wife of
a month, the laughing-stock of the hotel. We do not
pretend the man was altogether devoid of good im-
pulses; but the evil of his nature was strong—the
good feeble. He was ungrateful, heartless, unprin-
cipled. Evelyn had before known only the reverse
of the picture; she had been adored, petted, spoiled.
How could she conceive so exceptional a character

as that of Sir Percy?　How bear with him?　Dear
friends, she did bear with him, and she was not
wretched, for she now knew that all trials are the
just retribution for past sins committed, past duties
unperformed.　Alas! we cannot escape the past,
still does it pursue us like an avenging spectre;
and so she resolved to endure all, looking no
longer to earth for bliss, living ever in the
sweet calm and beauty of the inner life, which
proceeds from the Christ who shines on the souls
of all who will receive him as the pure and perfect law.

No longer spell-bound by her passionate love for
D'Arcy, he was yet dear—dearer to her than ever,
for to him alone she owed all her strength to bear, all
her courage to do; through him she had been enabled
to behold the radiant, the immeasureable life of the
beyond, as the one great reality of our being,
compared to which this earth life, did it last a
century, is but as a span, a point in eternity, "a
dream when one awaketh."　Oh, had she realized these blessed truths in earliest youth, how
different might have been her fate!　But, re-
pulsed by narrow-minded sectarianism, miscalled religion, she had strayed without a guide
in devious paths.

The idea of a future existence had then loomed darkly before her young imaginations as a vague terror, a portentous and lurid superstition forcing her to an unwilling lip-service of prayer. Now it was a glorious inspiration — hourly influencing her, and turning the common incidents of life into occasions for thanksgiving.

For she knew that the Infinite Father was calling his erring child home through her loves and through her griefs.

With this sweet conviction can tribulation harm her? I trow not. Rather do her crosses and her trials cause her lonely and unsatisfied heart to rise each day more purely, tenderly, devotedly, upward towards God. Then, too, she tremblingly believes she may, in a brighter sphere, be united in the sweet connubial tie to one who shall fully realize the ideal of her soul. So, loving and beloved, she will no longer dwell

> 'As one companionless
> In essence, heart distressed and pining ever
> With anguished yearning for a tenderness
> Forever widely sought, experienced never."*

---

* "Lyric of the Golden Age," by Rev. T. L. Harris.

Is she mistaken? I cannot think so. Is it possible to form too exalted an idea of the joys "God hath prepared for them that love him," which, we are told, "it hath not entered into the heart of man to conceive?" Yet, we may faintly shadow those ecstatic raptures, if we remember that every faculty of the mind, each affection of the spirit, will then be fully and forever occupied in fulfilling its highest destinies—LOVE, KNOWLEDGE, USE.* Sublime trinity! Such the occupations of the angels throughout eternity; and for those who here exercise themselves in these Christian graces, heaven has already begun on earth!

Nor do these truly catholic doctrines militate against a life of activity here — they are rather anti-monastic—teaching that the life of the body is necessary for the soul, and that the happiness of the spirit hereafter will be proportionate to the use we make of all our faculties and talents in the terrestrial state; while the contrary must be expected in the world of spirits, from a life of idleness; truly blessed they

> "in this loud stunning tide
> Of human care and crime,
> With whom the melodies abide

---

* See Swedenborg's works; also, "Arcana of Christianity," by Rev. T. L. Harris.

Of th' everlasting chime ;
Who carry music in their heart
Through dusky lane and wrangling mart,
Plying their daily task with busier feet,
Because their secret souls a holier strain repeat."*

* " Keble's Christian Year."

CHAPTER XXVII.

FIFTH AVENUE HOTEL.

LADY MONTGOMERY'S DIARY.

New York, Aug. 10*th.*—Seated in the window
of our parlor, I once more write my thoughts in my
journal. The wind is sultry—scarce a movement
stirs the trees in Madison Square, although the sun
has long since sunk below the horizon. Mary is play-
ing Chopin's music on a fine piano of Chickering's,
sent here to wait our arrival—a graceful attention
from Philip D'Arcy. I have just implored dear
Mary to repeat that Impromptu, to which the twilight lends additional charm. Oh! how infinitely
do I prefer instrumental to vocal music, especially
to the conventionalism of the modern school of Italian singing; even when the latter is well executed,
(which is rare) you know each intonation which
will be given; all is too material, it chains you down

to its own level—while the listening to a classical instrumental symphony is like following a long, closely-connected chain of reasoning, and at the same time you are inspired with a thousand new ideas and sensations; or the phrases of musical diction accompany you in the train of thought you are at the time pursuing—brightening, poetizing all. How I love to wander with the serious, philosophic Beethoven, through mazes of tangled modulations, at the same time clear and intricate, to revel in the delicious harmonized melodies of the divine Mozart, to drink in the weird and plaintive tones of the melancholy Weber, to muse, and sigh with the poet *pianiste* Chopin, criticising naught, analyzing naught, floating as it were, in an ocean of sweet sounds, lost in a reverie of ineffable bliss. Oh! if our most intense and delicious emotions are those of the mind, the spirit, who can say that the individual perishes with the worthless clay of the body!

11*th*.—I had written thus far when Philip D'Arcy entered, unexpected—unannounced. Oh! sweet surprise! if partings here are painful, there is at least compensation in again meeting those we love, when the charm of their dear presence is as sunlight after storm, as rest to the weary—as the fragrance of spring flowers after the snows of winter. In D'Arcy especially, as I have before mentioned, this power of fascination is remarkable; he enters, and your very soul is illumined with gladness, he departs, and a shadow falls on all around. Softly, tenderly, happily, we conversed in the dim twilight, the three I love most on earth.

Sir Percy was from home—he is rarely with us—D'Arcy expressed the desire to make my husband's acquaintance. *My husband*, how strangely from his lips did those words grate on my ear.

Aug. 15th.—Since I last wrote in my diary, only a few days have elapsed, and yet what events! It appears to me, as if I had dreamed a horrible dream and have at last awaked. We had decided on leaving the city on the morrow, escorted by D'Arcy, for his beautiful villa on the Hudson. Sir Percy, was, as usual, out—but Philip determined to wait his return in order to see him, and arrange with him about our journey—as yet they had never met.

Mary had retired early, feeling unwell, but at my request Ella remained to await with us Sir Percy's appearance. At about eleven we heard his heavy step in the corridor, and he entered the room.

" What, not yet in bed ?" he said.

" I waited," I replied, " to present you——"

The sentence was never finished, for at this moment D'Arcy emerged from the shadow, into the full glare of the gas-light. I saw Sir Percy stagger, as a drunken man, and turn almost pale. Thinking him ill, I would have sprung towards him, but Philip caught my wrist and held it as in a vice. I turned to look at him. To say that hatred and scorn flashed from his eyes were little, his entire form seemed dilated with passion, his eyes glowed and flamed like live coals, his lip and nostril expressed the most profound contempt.

The baronet, on the other hand, seemed paralyzed with terror; his fingers worked, and his hands trembled fearfully; his eyes (never able to support a look without flinching), now rolled in restless agony. D'Arcy paused only for a moment, as the tiger before his deadly spring—then, with one bound he cleared the space between himself and his victim: "Oh! cursed, cursed serpent," he muttered, between his clenched teeth, "how darest thou defile this pure Eden with the foul slime of thy presence? Demon in human form," and the delicate and spiritual-looking man shook his sturdy and muscular adversary as a reed, "demon, I say, how darest thou violate the sanctity of this angel home. Vile, pitiless wretch, where is poor Alice Vivian? Answer, if thy lying tongue can frame one word of truth, didst thou not wed her, break her heart, drive her to madness, and then shut her up with gibbering maniacs in a madhouse? and now she lives—no denial, I say," (as the hardened culprit made a movement of dissent), "she lives! by Heaven, she lives, thy wronged, thy wretched wife; a wreck in soul as in body. Oh! may the curse of a desolate heart and blighted affections recoil upon thee, may rest forsake thy pillow, and peace be forever a stranger to thy couch, that thy hard heart may be shivered at last, as into fragments, by blank despair — despair of pity here, of mercy hereafter! May God himself be deaf to the prayers wrung from thy bitter agony. No, go—I will not blaspheme: if thou bee'st a devil I cannot kill thee. Go, miserable man, and repent —if thou canst."

D'Arcy still held the cowed and trembling wretch in his nervous grasp. Ella, pale, almost fainting, had quitted the room. Silent, motionless, horror-stricken, with dilated eyes, I watched, as in a nightmare, the fearful scene, powerless to speak or scream. I saw Philip at length open the door, violently ejecting, almost flinging the man from the room. I saw no more—my trembling limbs refused any longer to sustain me. I sank into the nearest chair, sick—sick, covering my face with my hands, a film before my eyes. On recovering consciousness, I was alone, and all was still.

CHAPTER XXVIII.

SHADOWS.

ELLA TO PHILIP D'ARCY.

The Retreat, September ——, 18——.

FORGIVE me for what I am about to write. Indeed, I feel that I am performing a duty, even though my dear mother is ignorant of this step. I must, however, add, that I have the full approbation of one who never fails to judge rightly—I mean our good, sensible friend, Mary Mildmay. Dear Mr. D'Arcy, esteeming and respecting you above all men living, as I do, you will think it strange, when I tell you that I have come to the conclusion, seriously and advisedly, that I can *never* be your wife; and, believe me, this resolution is *irrevocable*. As a favor, I implore you not to attempt to change my determination. It would be

utterly fruitless. Would you know my reasons?
They are many.

When you honored me, by asking my hand, I
was a mere child. I am now a woman, and must
exert the prerogative of my sex—that of choice—in
a matter which concerns my own happiness, and
your future welfare. Know, then, that I am inspired to say to you, that, in marrying me, you
will *pass by your destiny.* The impression is so
strong that I cannot, if I would, shake it off; but
must obey, as if a voice from heaven had spoken.
Do you not know, too, that I have sworn never to
forsake my beloved mother in her sorrow and her
loneliness? And can I falsify my oath? In order
to remove all further doubt from your mind, know,
likewise, that it is not to *me* that you owe your life.
Poor little Ella nursed you tenderly, it is true,
through your convalescence; but it was her dear
mother who recalled you, by the magnetism of her
health-producing touch, from the trance of death;
and, in so doing, she herself nearly perished. If I
have yet another reason for thus writing—*that* I
must ever preserve profoundly secret.

One parting favor I request: let this make no
difference. Come to us as before. Be still a friend—
prove thus to me that I have your pardon—for-

give—forget. Yes, forget all, except that I shall
never cease to pray for your happiness, and that
     I am, as ever,
       Your affectionate friend,
            ELLA.

My readers may readily imagine how highly I
approved my young friend's dignified and womanly
letter. I had never thought them suited either in
years or in tastes. Ella, lovely, sweet, innocent,
intelligent, was yet scarcely the companion required
by a man of D'Arcy's intellect and superior mind.
Their temperaments, too, were similar, each being
outwardly cold, reserved, calm, unimpulsive. Now
I have invariably found that the happiest unions
proceed from similarity of taste, but diversity of
temperament. I was therefore satisfied as to the wis-
dom of my Ella's decision. We had now been
staying about a fortnight in this lovely place, where
D'Arcy, on the plea of very pressing business at
Washington, had excused himself from escorting
us. He had, however, sent his confidential servant
with us, as courier, having telegraphed to his house-
keeper to have all in readiness on our arrival at
" the Retreat." And in truth the house was furnished with a luxury only to be attained by the
union of refined taste with great wealth in its

owner. We discerned the ever-presiding hand of affection in the recently-arrived harp and piano, and in the works of modern literature, and late numbers of periodicals which filled the shelves, and encumbered the tables of the sitting-rooms. Some men never remember anything—D'Arcy had that double memory of heart and head which never forgets the most minute arrangement or least matured intention. Poor Evelyn, humiliated, heart-broken at the wicked deception which had been practiced upon her, loathing her position of reputed wife to such a villain, was glad to hide her burning sense of shame in complete solitude, happy even, that D'Arcy, in respectful sympathy, delicately kept aloof for a time. The latter had not yet replied to Ella's letter, but in about ten days he wrote to Evelyn a few lines, expressing the fear that business might detain him another month at Washington, but that the moment he could hope for a few days' recreation, he would visit his friends at "The Retreat." He hinted a fear that he had alarmed herself and her sweet Ella, and asked pardon if his uncontrollable indignation had caused him to forget for the first time what is due to the presence of ladies. This slight allusion was the only one he made to having received Ella's letter of dismissal. Strange Being, and unlike all others, I thought!—

And the days passed onward, and Evelyn was made acquainted by her daughter that her engagement with D'Arcy was at an end, and the sad mother carefully scrutinized each look and movement of her child —for with the exaggeration of love, she could ill believe that one who had been chosen by Philip D'Arcy as his bride, could live without him, and be happy. So she tenderly watched lest the delicate rose should fade from that young cheek, lest the soft blue eyes should look dim, and lack their wonted lustre. It did strike me that the young girl's step was less elastic, and that she more frequently than was her wont, sought the solitude of her chamber. But I persuaded Evelyn that the shock experienced by poor Ella, on the discovery of Sir Percy's perfidious conduct, and her sympathy for her mother's now blighted life, sufficiently accounted for this apparent change in her.

And now the glorious Indian Summer pervades the atmosphere with a glowing and intense heat, the heavens wear a deeper tint of azure, the forests clothed in their Autumn foliage, varying from the palest shade of gold, and the softest green, to the richest and most brilliant scarlet, and the deepest crimson, remind you of the trees in the fabled garden of Aladdin, whose branches were pendant with the weight of rubies, emeralds, topaz and other precious stones, so wonderfully gorgeous are the November tints of the North American forests, so unlike anything ever beheld in the Old World. It seems almost as if nature, prophetic of coming decay, would array herself for the last time in her gayest and richest attire, and like Cleopatra of old queen it even on her couch of death.

And as one fine evening we sat in the verandah, enjoying the fresh breezes, and looking on the deep and rapid Hudson, we observed the splendid large steamer stop opposite the landing, and a few passengers enter the small boat which rowed towards shore. Listlessly we watched, soothed by the quiet beauty of the scene. A quarter of an hour may possibly have elapsed, when hearing the door open, we turned gladly to perceive and joyfully welcome Philip D'Arcy.

CHAPTER XXIX.

FOREGLEAMS.

It is evening; the air is soft and balmy, the gorgous sunset flushes the mountain tops, and falling on the gladsome river causes it to glitter like molten gold. The advancing steamer, heavy with its freight of human hearts, their loves and their cares, is enveloped in a glow of hazy light; the clear mirror of the crystal Hudson reflects the blue, unclouded expanse of the heavens. The acacias gently wave, and the aspens tenderly quiver in the languid air. A moment, and the amber sun sinks below the horizon, and white-robed twilight advances stealthily, as a holy nun bearing incense; softly she distils with fairy fingers, the sparkling dew-drops, and the water-lilies close their waxen petals, and the birds fold their weary wings, all but the nightingale, who ever maketh melody. Now the dragon-fly awakes, and the glancing fish make ripple on the water: the cricket chirps, and the glow-worm and

her sister, the fire-fly, prepare their tiny lamps. How
blissful a calm steals over the senses; what sweet
peace pervades the soul attuned to the harmonies of
nature. On such a night as this did Philip D'Arcy
and Evelyn wander forth in the clear obscure, their
feet sought the green paths where the cool moss grew
beside the bubbling streamlet, and the night flowers
wept beneath the silent stars, dreamily they saun-
tered side by side, their souls permeated with the
placid tenderness of that soft hour. They spoke not,
yet Evelyn felt through her entire being, the
passionate gaze of those deep eyes, and the delicious
consciousness that she was beloved glowed on her
cheek and caused her eyelids to droop in timid
emotion; they spake not, for they dared not break
the ineffable charm of that mute language. Yet
D'Arcy must leave that night, and he had much
to say, and Evelyn, by the instinct of love,
knew that he had much to say, and yet they
could not find it in their heart to break the spell,
the elysium of that silent hour. But Philip must
no longer keep silence, "Evelyn," he murmured
softly, and it was the first time he had thus named
her, "I know not how I shall support absence
from—from my friends—from you."

"You will return," she whispered.

"Return—ah! if God spare my life to happiness

—to love. Evelyn, forgive—pardon, my mistake; the fatal misapprehension, not of my heart—oh! do not think it; but I believed—I feared you loved another."

"*Never*, Philip! Oh! I know it now, too well!"

Then in words of burning eloquence, he poured forth the long restrained passion of his soul. He told how that she was the one love of his life; how that all past feelings were cold and worthless com pared to this; how his very being was entwined with hers; and kneeling at her feet he besought her to become his bride—his own.

Though the intense joy of that moment was almost an agony, Evelyn by a supreme effort mastering her agitation, besought her lover to rise, then she said, sadly, sorrowfully, tearfully, but with firmness:

"Too late—too late. Philip, this can never be."

"Never? Oh, God! Evelyn, do not jest. Can it be that after all, I am indifferent to you?"

She turned upon him a look of such fond, such devoted, such adoring love, that he would have caught her to his breast, but he dared not—so timid, so respectful, is true love.

"Philip, you are dear—dearer to me than existence. From the first moment I beheld you, you

have been the star of my destiny ; and yet, I repeat,
I never, never can be yours."

" And that lip, the very arch of Cupid's bow—
those perfect lips, where love in smiles and dimples
holds his throne—can they frame such cruel words.
Sweetest, this is no time for coquetry."

" Ah ! Philip, speak not of that fatal beauty which
has ever been my curse. Hear me with patience.
Your affection to me is beyond all price; but, yet,
far more do I prize your honor. Never, oh! never,
may the unwedded wife of Sir Percy Montgomery
become the bride of the noble, the peerless D'Arcy.
The world ——"

" What of that?" broke in Philip.

" Nothing, when we act rightly — everything
when we do wrong. Never through Evelyn shall
the heartless world have reason to cast a slur on the
fair fame of him she venerates above all men ; never shall it be said that his name is no longer untar-
nished. Philip, the mother of your once betrothed
can not, must not, name you husband. We must,
therefore, part."

" Part, Evelyn? In pity, say not so! My life—
my love—my bird of beauty—we will forsake the
haunts of men ; together will we fly to distant
climes—there, alone in the wilds of a yet virgin solitude, will we live each for the other only, and earth

shall become for us a second Eden. Say, sweet
one! shall it not be so?"

For one moment only did she waver. The idea
of such bliss was too intoxicating—her brain reeled
as in delirium. The temptation to give up all for
him was too strong. A moment, and she would
have sunk upon his breast, breathless, fainting, over-
come—when, suddenly, she seemed to behold, over
against the dark sycamore grove, the form of Ella—
her child—her first-born—her only one—the long
fair hair, dank and uncurled, floating in the dewy
night—the sweet young face pale and sad. The
semblance vanished: but, once more, Evelyn listened to her better angel. Self was forgotten—the
weakness past—the struggle over. Turning on her
beloved a look which he never ceased to remember—a look which consoled him in all troubles, and
which ever inspired him to noble deeds, because in
that pure glance earthly passion had given place to
celestial love, she said, gently, but decisively, and
without wavering—"We have both duties to per-
form; you will serve your country—be it mine to
protect my child, to soothe the suffering, to console
the afflicted. Ah! me—I have much to redeem in
the past."

"Cruel and unkind!—and since when have you
thus changed?"

"Since I have known you, Philip. All that is good in me I owe to you alone—and to you, next God, I look for strength and courage to persevere."

"And so help me Heaven, you shall not look in vain!" rejoined her lover, now restored to better feeling. "But must we part?"

"Yes—more than ever beloved—here for a time, to be united forever ere long, when made 'perfect through suffering,' we shall be found worthy to attain to the joys of angelhood. In the faith of this sweet hope, I can bear to part on earth for ever even from you."

Evelyn's eyes beamed with an almost supernatural radiance; and as the moon, bursting from forth a cloud that had momentarily veiled her splendor, shone full upon her chiselled features, she almost looked a denizen of that world to which she aspired. But the light of inspiration was soon quenched in tears of pardonable human sorrow; and, as Philip strained her to his wildly-throbbing heart, their lips met, and their souls blended in one long, long kiss—the first—the last—seal of their union for eternity. Surely the angels were present, and smiled benignantly on their pure and holy espousals.

CHAPTER XXX.

AND Philip has departed, and Evelyn is alone with the sweet memories of that thrice blessed eve, alone with her undying love, her high resolve. No, not alone, for ever in spirit she beholds deep within the pure and liquid wells of those beloved eyes, the fond gaze of unutterable tenderness, for ever she looks beyond this weary vale of tears, and sees in faith, the golden gates unclose through which the radiance of the Divine Sun streams downward, to enlighten the fields of care.

And moons have waxed and waned, and her Philip is now a General in the Federal Army, his name on every lip, his praise on every tongue. And thus it must ever be. Men must DO great and heroic deeds—and we must ENDURE and SUFFER. Which is the truer heroism? But we, too, may look beyond, and upward to the ever present ONE who, if during the Divine Humanity of His earth life, He had occasion, not unfrequently, to rebuke the errors and falsities of mankind, was ever tender and compassionate to the faults and failings of woman.

Oh! my sisters—" Be ye also merciful, as He is merciful."

THE END.

1863.

A NEW LIST OF

BOOKS

ISSUED BY

CARLETON, PUBLISHER,

(LATE RUDD & CARLETON,)

413 Broadway,

NEW YORK.

NEW BOOKS

And New Editions Recently Issued by

CARLETON, PUBLISHER,

(Late RUDD & CARLETON,)

413 *BROADWAY, NEW YORK.*

Les Miserables.

Victor Hugo's great novel—the only complete unabridged translation. Library Edition. Five vols. 12mo. cloth, each, $1.00.

The same, five vols. 8vo. cloth, $1.00.   Paper covers, 50 cts.

The same, (cheap ed.) 1 vol. 8vo. cloth, $1.50. paper, $1.00.

Les Miserables—Illustrations.

26 photographic illustrations, by Brion.   Elegant quarto, $3.00

Among the Pines,

or, Down South in Secession Time. Cloth, $1.00, paper, 75 cts.

My Southern Friends.

By author of "Among the Pines." Cloth, $1.00. paper, 75 cts.

Rutledge.

A powerful American novel, by an unknown author, $1.50.

The Sutherlands.

The new novel by the popular author of "Rutledge," $1.50.

The Habits of Good Society.

A hand-book for ladies and gentlemen. Best, wittiest, most entertaining work on taste and good manners ever printed, $1.50

The Cloister and the Hearth.

A magnificent new historical novel, by Charles Reade, author of "Peg Woffington," etc., cloth, $1.50, paper covers, $1.25.

Beulah.

A novel of remarkable power, by Miss A. J. Evans. $1.50.

Artemus Ward, His Book.
The racy writings of this humorous author. Illustrated, $1.25.

The Old Merchants of New York.
Entertaining reminiscences of ancient mercantile New York City, by " Walter Barrett, clerk." First Series. $1.50 each.

Like and Unlike.
Novel by A. S. Roe, author of " I've been thinking," &c. $1 50.

Orpheus C. Kerr Papers.
Second series of letters by this comic military authority. $1.25.

Marian Grey.
New domestic novel, by the author of " Lena Rivers," etc. $1.50.

Lena Rivers.
A popular American novel, by Mrs. Mary J. Holmes, $1.50.

A Book about Doctors.
An entertaining volume about the medical profession. $1.50.

The Adventures of Verdant Green.
Humorous novel of English College life. Illustrated. $1.25.

The Culprit Fay.
Joseph Rodman Drake's faery poem, elegantly printed, 50 cts.

Doctor Antonio.
A charming love-tale of Italian life, by G. Ruffini, $1.50.

Lavinia.
A new love-story, by the author of " Doctor Antonio," $1.50.

Dear Experience.
An amusing Parisian novel, by author " Doctor Antonio," $1.00.

The Life of Alexander Von Humboldt.
A new and popular biography of this *savant*, including his travels and labors, with introduction by Bayard Taylor, $1.50.

Love (L'Amour.)
A remarkable volume, from the French of Michelet. $1.25.

Woman (La Femme.)
A continuation of " Love (L'Amour)," by same author, $1.25.

The Sea (La Mer.)
New work by Michelet, author " Love" and " Woman," $1.25.

The Moral History of Woman.
Companion to Michelet's " L'Amour," from the French, $1.25

Mother Goose for Grown Folks.
Humorous and satirical rhymes for grown people, 75 cts.

The Kelly's and the O'Kelly's.
Novel by Anthony Trollope, author of " Doctor Thorne," $1.50.

The Great Tribulation.

Or, Things coming on the earth, by Rev. John Cumming, D.D., author "Apocalyptic Sketches," etc., two series, each $1.00.

The Great Preparation.

Or, Redemption draweth nigh, by Rev. John Cumming, D.D., author "The Great Tribulation," etc., two series, each $1.00.

The Great Consummation.

Sequel "Great Tribulation," Dr. Cumming, two series, $1.00.

Teach us to Pray.

A new work on The Lord's Prayer, by Dr. Cumming, $1.00.

The Slave Power.

By Jas. E. Cairnes, of Dublin University, Lond. ed. $1.25.

Game Fish of the North.

A sporting work for Northern States and Canada. Illus., $1.50.

Drifting About.

By Stephen C. Massett ("Jeemes Pipes"), illustrated, $1.25

The Flying Dutchman.

A humorous Poem by John G. Saxe, with illustrations, 50 cts.

Notes on Shakspeare.

By Jas. H. Hackett, the American Comedian (portrait), $1.50.

The Spirit of Hebrew Poetry.

By Isaac Taylor, author "History of Enthusiasm," etc., $2.00.

A Life of Hugh Miller.

Author of "Testimony of the Rocks," &c., new edition, $1.50.

A Woman's Thoughts about Women.

By Miss Dinah Mulock, author of "John Halifax," etc., $1.00.

Curiosities of Natural History.

An entertaining vol., by F. T. Buckland ; two series, each $1.25.

The Partisan Leader.

Beverley Tucker's notorious Southern Disunion novel, $1.25.

Cesar Birotteau.

First of a series of Honore de Balzac's best French novels, $1.00.

Petty Annoyances of Married Life.

The second of the series of Balzac's best French novels, $1.00.

The Alchemist.

The third of the series of the best of Balzac's novels, $1.00.

Eugenie Grandet.

The fourth of the series of Balzac's best French novels, $1.00.

The National School for the Soldier.

Elementary work for the soldier ; by Capt. Van Ness, 50 cts.

Tom Tiddler's Ground.
Charles Dickens's new Christmas Story, paper cover,   25 cts.

National Hymns.
An essay by Richard Grant White.   8vo. embellished, $1.00.

George Brimley.
Literary Essays reprinted from the British Quarterlies, $1.25

Thomas Bailey Aldrich.
First complete collection of Poems, blue and gold binding, $1.00.

Out of His Head.
A strange and eccentric romance by T. B. Aldrich, $1.00.

The Course of True Love
Never did run smooth.   A Poem by Thomas B. Aldrich, 50 cts.

Poems of a Year.
By Thomas B. Aldrich, author of "Babie Bell," &c.,   75 cts.

The King's Bell.
A Mediæval Legend in verse, by R. H. Stoddard,   75 cts.

The Morgesons.
A clever novel of American Life, by Mrs. R. H. Stoddard, $1.00.

Beatrice Cenci.
An historical novel by F. D. Guerrazzi, from the Italian, $1.50.

Isabella Orsini.
An historical novel by the author of "Beatrice Cenci," $1.25.

A Popular Treatise on Deafness.
For individuals and families, by E. B. Lighthill, M.D., $1.00.

Oriental Harems and Scenery.
A gossipy work, translated from the French of Belgiojoso, $1.25.

Lola Montez.
Her lectures and autobiography, with a steel portrait, $1.25.

John Doe and Richard Roe.
A novel of New York city life, by Edward S. Gould, $1.00.

Doesticks' Letters.
The original letters of this great humorist, illustrated, $1.50.

Plu-ri-bus-tah.
A comic history of America, by "Doesticks," illus., $1.50.

The Elephant Club.
A humorous description of club-life, by "Doesticks," $1.50.

Vernon Grove.
A novel by Mrs. Caroline H. Glover, Charleston, S. C., $1.00.

The Book of Chess Literature.
A complete Encyclopædia of this subject, by D. W. Fiske, $1.50.

Tactics.
Or, Cupid in Shoulder-straps. A West Point love story, $1.00.

Sprees and Splashes.
A volume of humorous sketches, by Henry Morford, $1.00.

Around the Pyramids.
A new book of adventure and travel, by Aaron Ward, $1.25.

Garret Van Horn.
Or, The Beggar on Horseback, by John S. Sauzade, $1.25.

Aisio Balzani.
Or, The Diary of a Proscribed Sicilian, by D. Minnelli, $1.25.

China and the Chinese.
Being recent personal reminiscences, by W. L. G. Smith, $1.25.

Transition.
A Memoir of Emma Whiting, by Rev. H. S. Carpenter, $1.00.

Lulu.
A novel of Life in Washington, by M. T. Walworth, $1.25.

Lyrics and Idyls.
"Diamond Wedding," and other poems, by E. C. Stedman, 75 cts.

The Prince's Ball.
A humorous poem by Edmund C. Stedman, illustrated, 50 cts.

Gen. Nathaniel Lyon.
The life and political writings of the late patriot soldier, $1.00.

Twenty Years around the World.
Volume of travel, by John Guy Vassar, Poughkeepsie, $2.50.

Philip Thaxter.
A new novel, with scenes in California, one vol. 12mo., $1.00.

From Haytime to Hopping.
A novel by the author of "Our Farm of Four Acres," $1.00.

Fast Day Sermons.
Of 1861, the best Sermons by the prominent Divines, $1.25.

Debt and Grace.
The Doctrine of a Future Life, by Rev. C. F. Hudson, $1.25.

Fort Lafayette.
A novel, by the Hon. Benjamin Wood, of New York, $1.00.

Romance of a Poor Young Man.
A capital novel from the French of Octave Feuillet, $1.00.

Sarah Gould.
Volume of miscellaneous poems, bound in blue and gold, 75 cts.

The Monitor.
A new book of travel, by Wm. Hoffman, illustrated, $1.50.

England in Rhyme.
A pleasant method for instructing children in History, 50 cts.

Brown's Carpenter's Assistant.
A practical work on architecture, with plans, large 4to., $5.00.

Sybelle
And other miscellaneous poems, by L——, 12mo., cloth, 75 cts

Wa-Wa-Wanda.
A legend of old Orange County, New York, in verse, 75 cts.

Husband vs. Wife.
A satirical poem, by Henry Clapp, Jr., illus. by Hoppin, 60 cts.

Roumania.
Travels in Eastern Europe, by J. O. Noyes, illustrated, $1.50.

The Christmas Tree.
A volume of miscellany for the young, with illustrations, 75 cts.

The Captive Nightingale.
A charming little book for children, many illustrations, 75 cts.

Sunshine through the Clouds.
Comprising stories for juveniles, beautifully illustrated, 75 cts.

Cosmogony,
Or, the mysteries of creation, by Thomas A. Davies, $1.50.

An Answer to Hugh Miller
And other kindred geologists, by Thomas A. Davies, $1.25.

Walter Ashwood.
A novel by "Paul Siogvolk," author of "Schediasms," $1.00.

Southwold.
A new society novel by Mrs. Lillie Devereux Umsted, $1.00.

Ballads of the War.
A collection of poems for 1861, by George W. Hewes, 75 cts.

Hartley Norman.
A new and striking American novel; one large 12mo., $1.25.

The Vagabond.
Sketches on literature, art, and society, by Adam Badeau, $1.00

Edgar Poe and His Critics.
A literary critique by Mrs. Sarah Helen Whitman,   75 cts.

The New and the Old.
Sketches in California and India, by Dr. J. W. Palmer, $1.25

Up and Down the Irrawaddi.
Adventures in the Burman Empire, by J. W. Palmer, $1.00.

Miles Standish Illustrated.
With photographs, by J. W. Ehninger, elegant 4to., $6.00.